WITH
Pea, Bee, & Jay
WANNABEES

Brian "Smitty" Smith

HARPER
alley

An Imprint of HarperCollinsPublishers

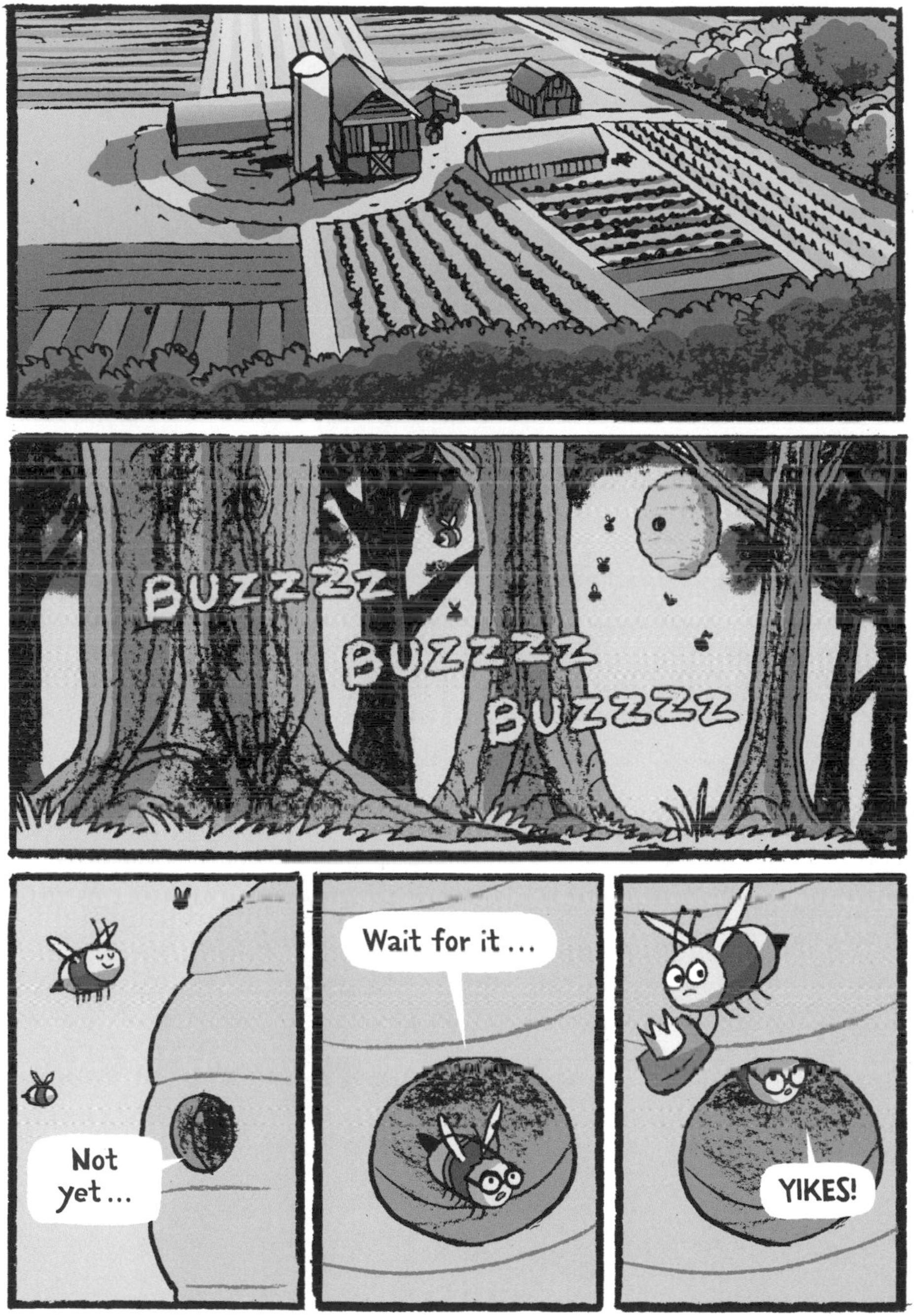
BUZZZZ
BUZZZZ
BUZZZZ
Not yet...
Wait for it...
YIKES!

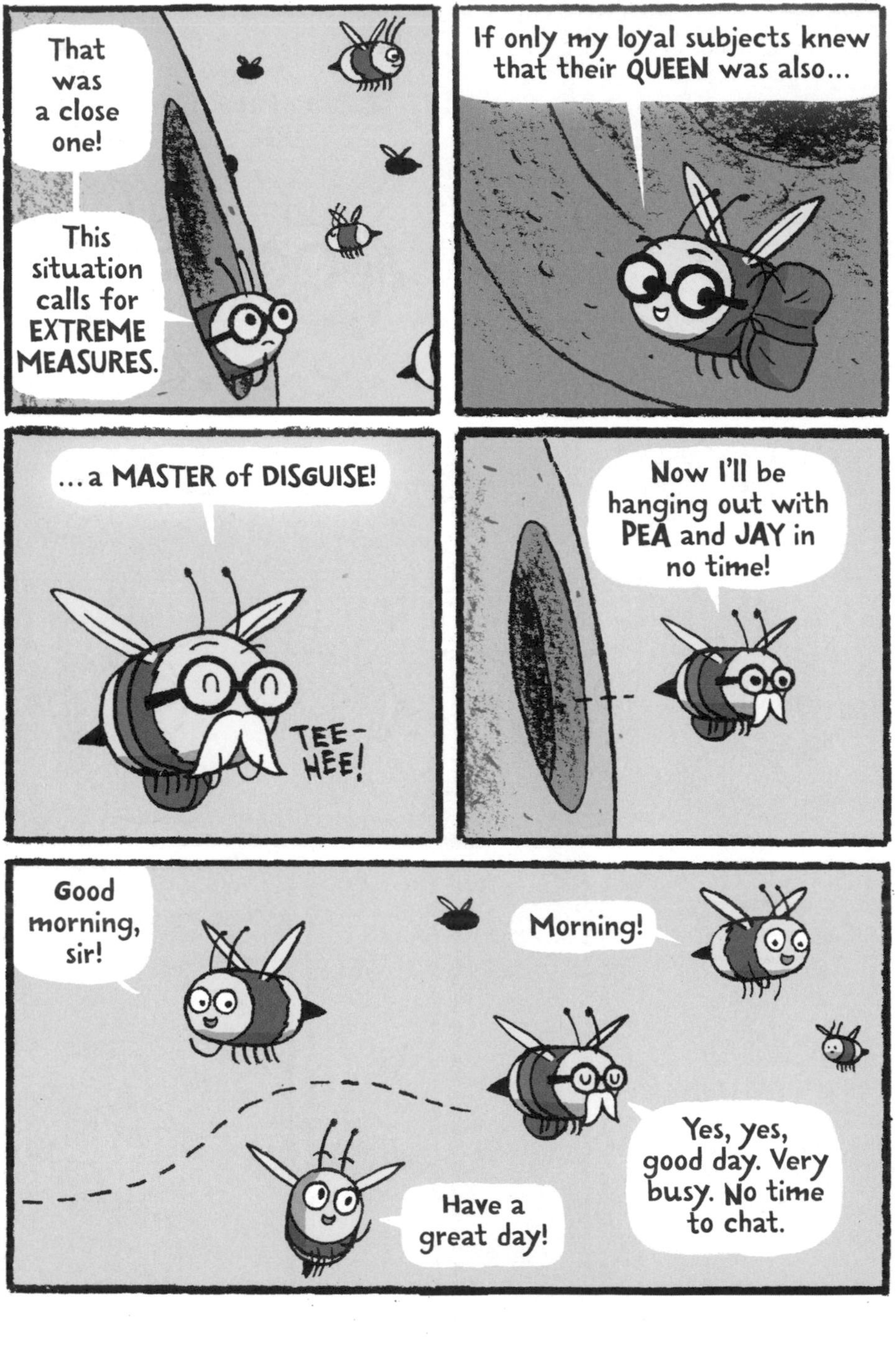

That was a close one!
This situation calls for EXTREME MEASURES.
If only my loyal subjects knew that their QUEEN was also...
... a MASTER of DISGUISE!
TEE-HEE!
Now I'll be hanging out with PEA and JAY in no time!
Good morning, sir!
Morning!
Yes, yes, good day. Very busy. No time to chat.
Have a great day!

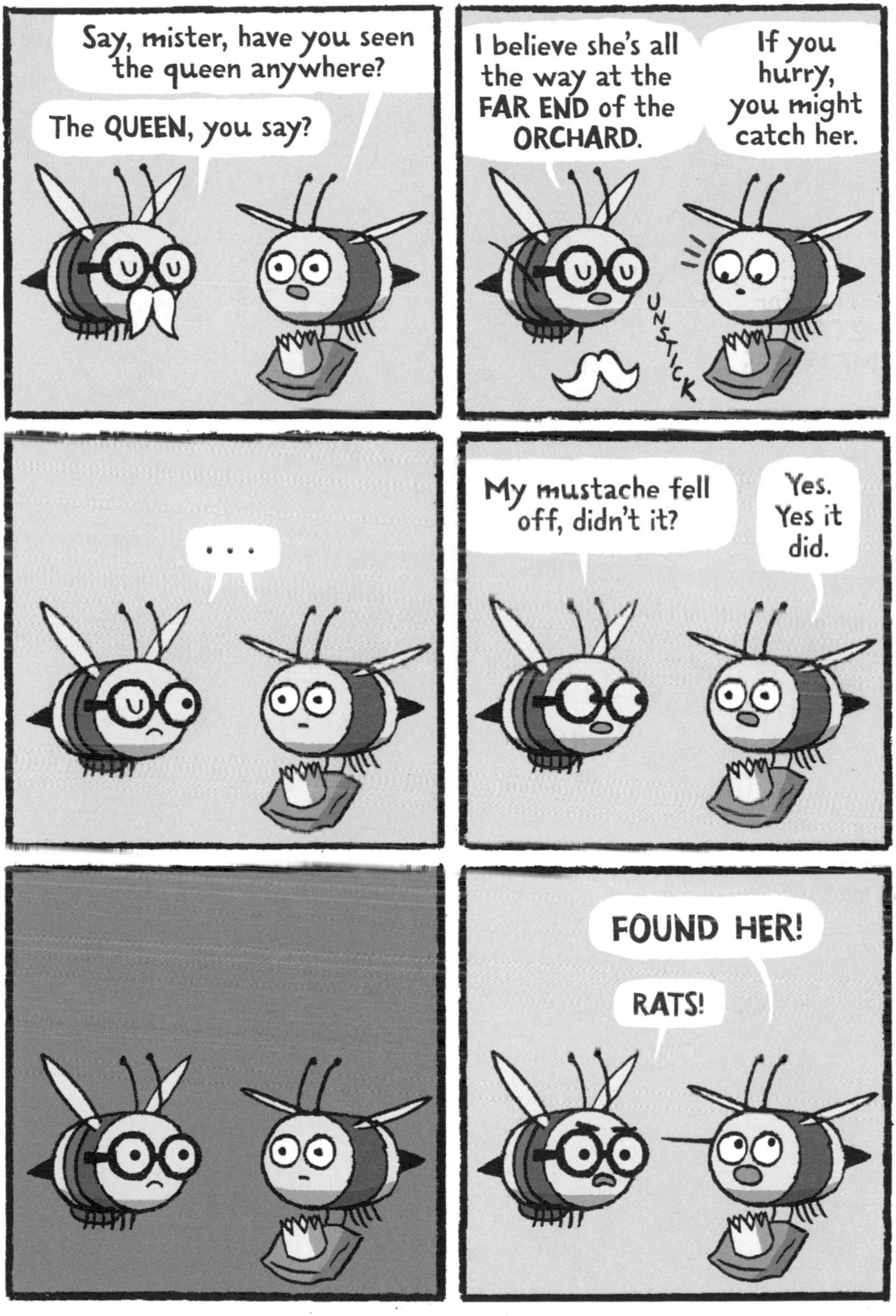
Say, mister, have you seen the queen anywhere?
The QUEEN, you say?
I believe she's all the way at the FAR END of the ORCHARD.
If you hurry, you might catch her.
UNSTICK
. . .
My mustache fell off, didn't it?
Yes. Yes it did.
FOUND HER!
RATS!

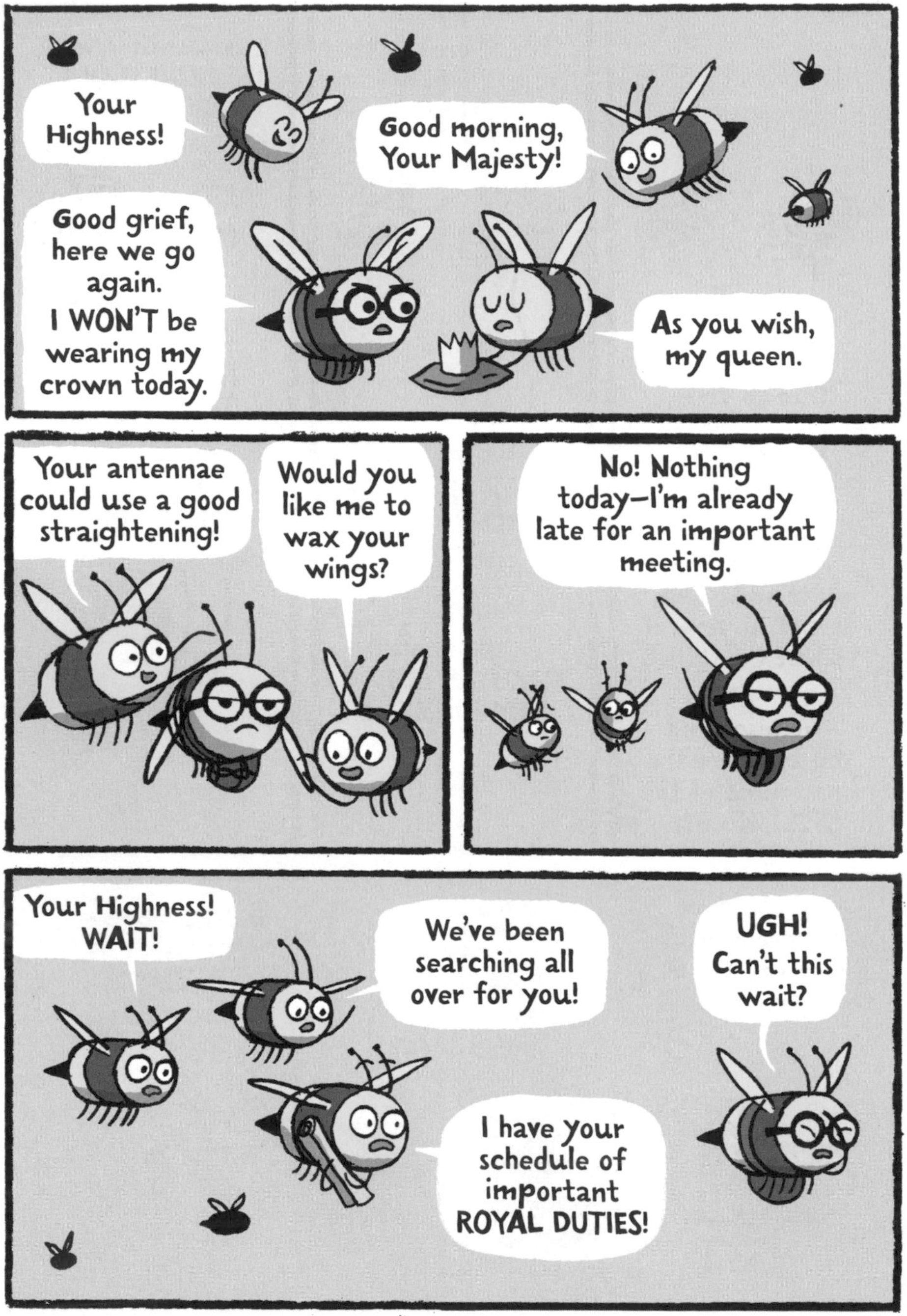
Your Highness!
Good morning, Your Majesty!
Good grief, here we go again. I WON'T be wearing my crown today.
As you wish, my queen.
Your antennae could use a good straightening!
Would you like me to wax your wings?
No! Nothing today—I'm already late for an important meeting.
Your Highness! WAIT!
We've been searching all over for you!
I have your schedule of important ROYAL DUTIES!
UGH! Can't this wait?

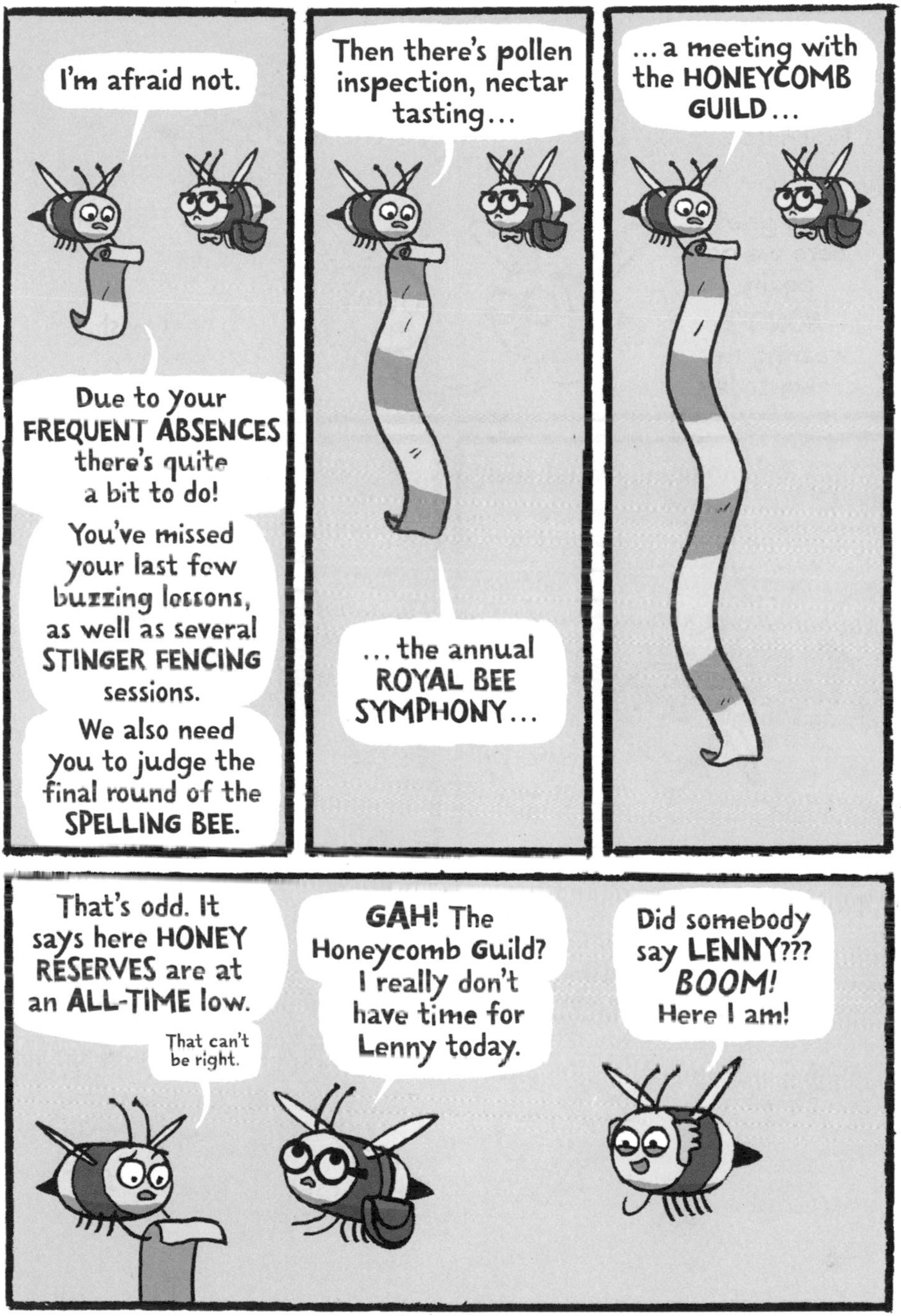
I'm afraid not.
Due to your FREQUENT ABSENCES there's quite a bit to do!
You've missed your last few buzzing lessons, as well as several STINGER FENCING sessions.
We also need you to judge the final round of the SPELLING BEE.
Then there's pollen inspection, nectar tasting...
... the annual ROYAL BEE SYMPHONY...
... a meeting with the HONEYCOMB GUILD...
That's odd. It says here HONEY RESERVES are at an ALL-TIME low.
That can't be right.
GAH! The Honeycomb Guild? I really don't have time for Lenny today.
Did somebody say LENNY??? BOOM! Here I am!

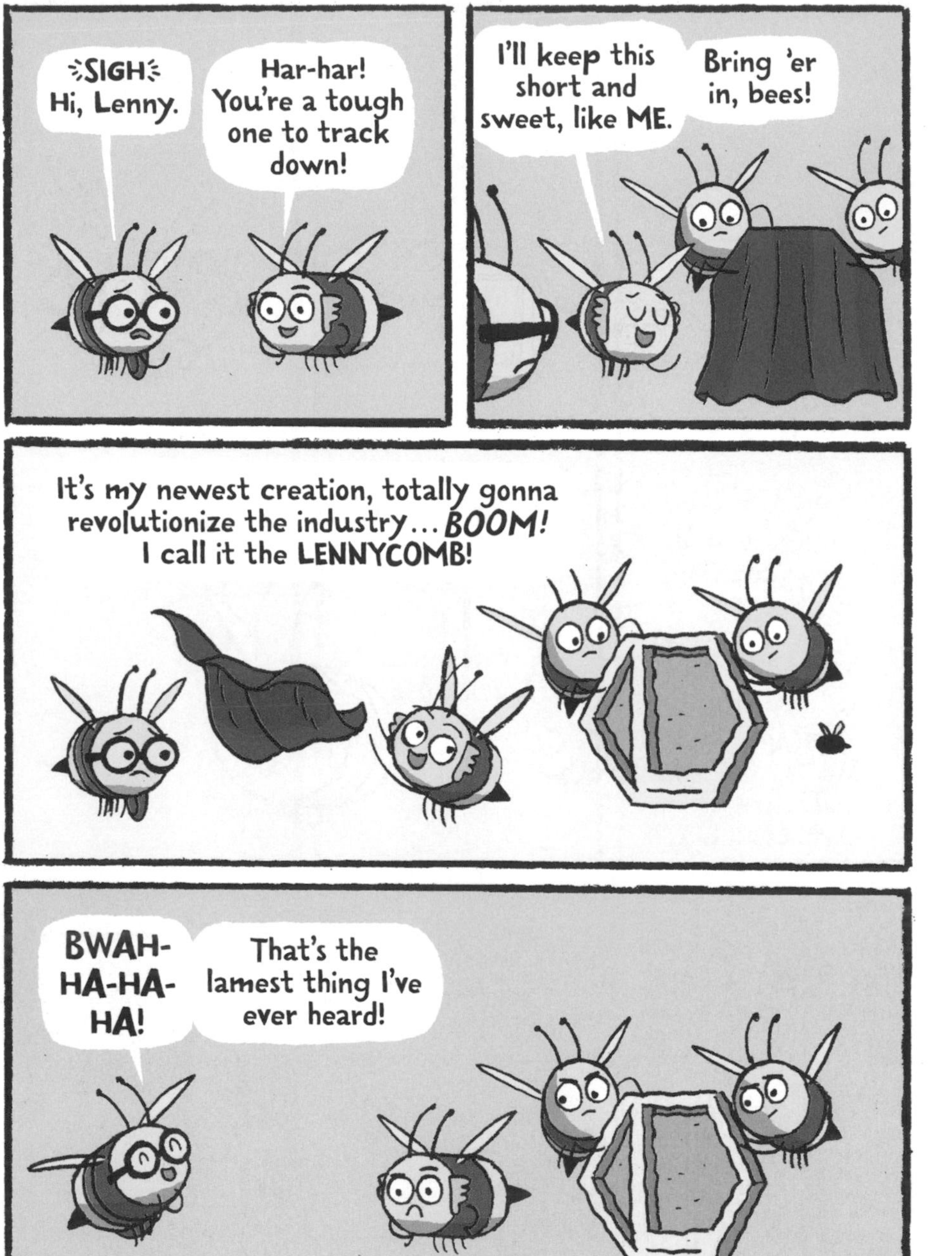
SIGH
Hi, Lenny.
Har-har! You're a tough one to track down!
I'll keep this short and sweet, like ME.
Bring 'er in, bees!
It's my newest creation, totally gonna revolutionize the industry... BOOM! I call it the LENNYCOMB!
BWAH-HA-HA-HA!
That's the lamest thing I've ever heard!

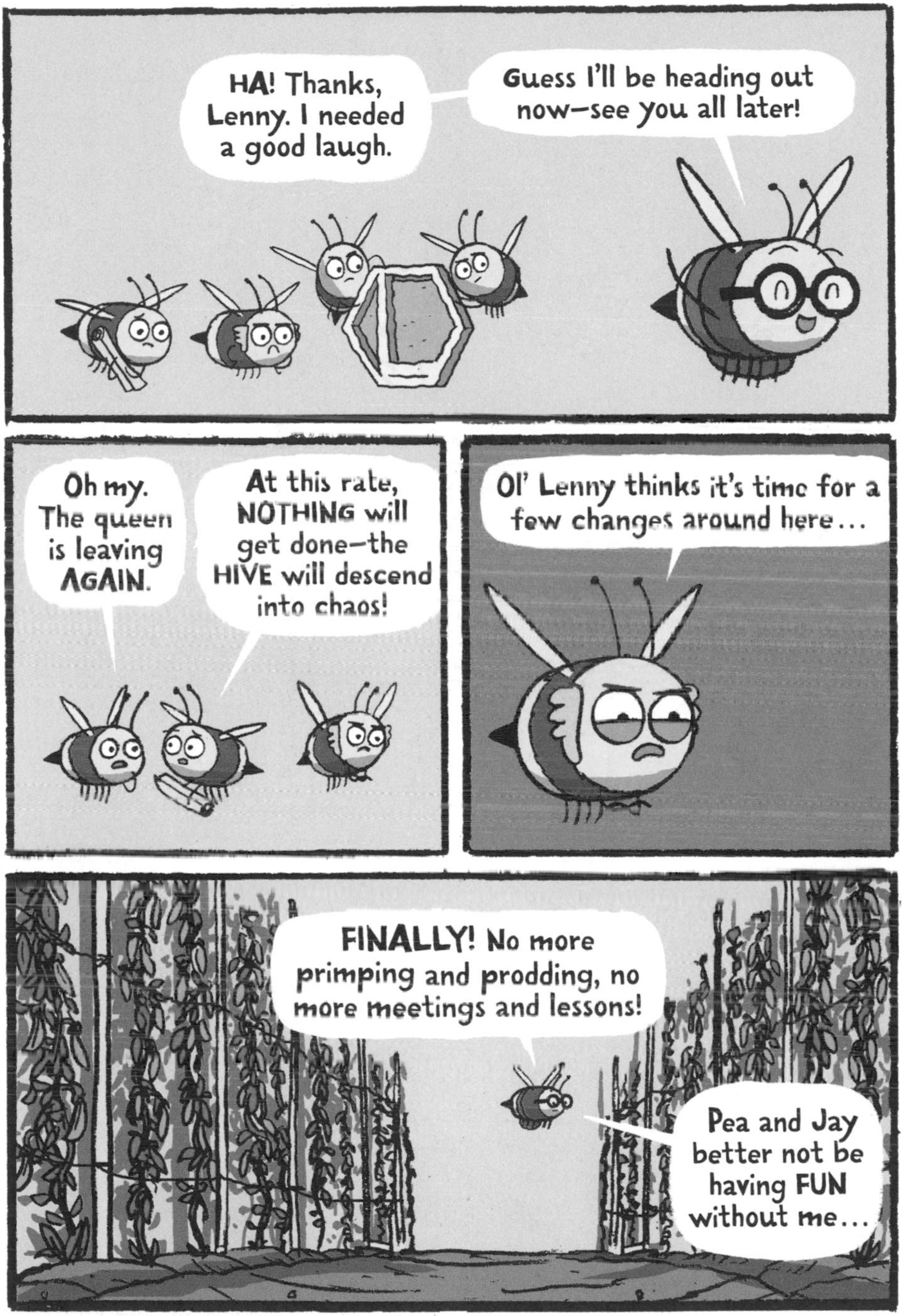
HA! Thanks, Lenny. I needed a good laugh.
Guess I'll be heading out now—see you all later!
Oh my. The queen is leaving AGAIN.
At this rate, NOTHING will get done—the HIVE will descend into chaos!
Ol' Lenny thinks it's time for a few changes around here...
FINALLY! No more primping and prodding, no more meetings and lessons!
Pea and Jay better not be having FUN without me...

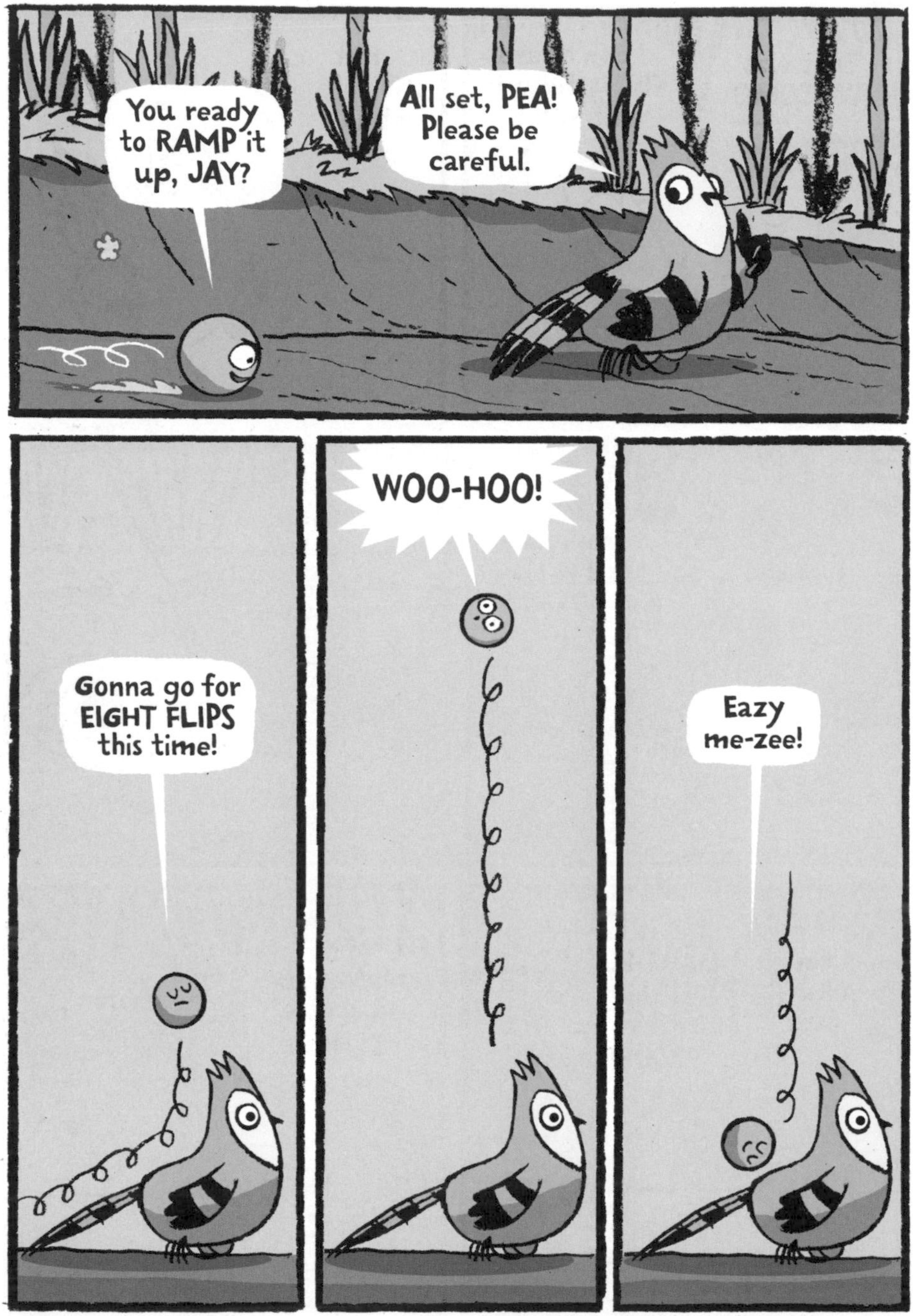
You ready to RAMP it up, JAY?
All set, PEA! Please be careful.
Gonna go for EIGHT FLIPS this time!
WOO-HOO!
Eazy me-zee!

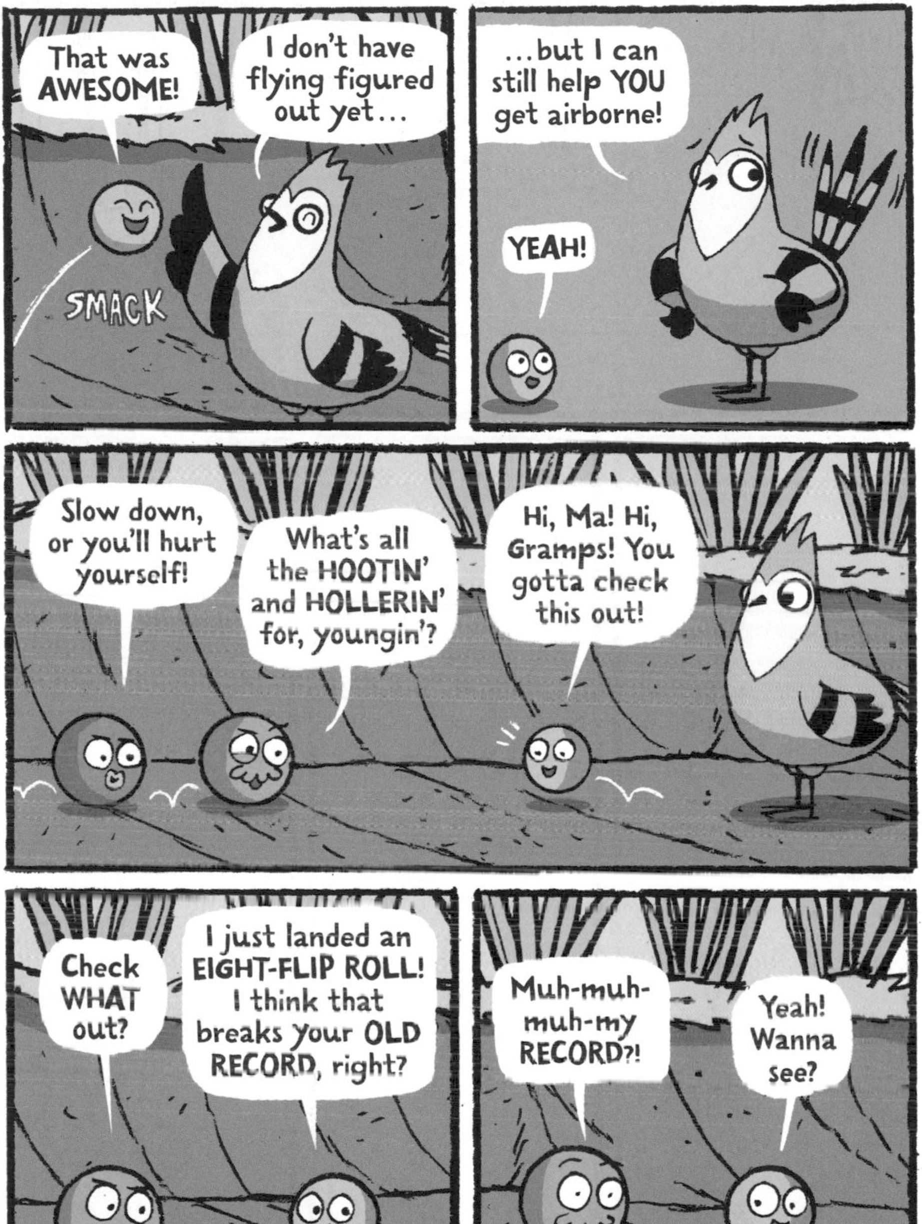
That was AWESOME!
I don't have flying figured out yet...
SMACK
...but I can still help YOU get airborne!
YEAH!
Slow down, or you'll hurt yourself!
What's all the HOOTIN' and HOLLERIN' for, youngin'?
Hi, Ma! Hi, Gramps! You gotta check this out!
Check WHAT out?
I just landed an EIGHT-FLIP ROLL! I think that breaks your OLD RECORD, right?
Muh-muh-muh-my RECORD?!
Yeah! Wanna see?

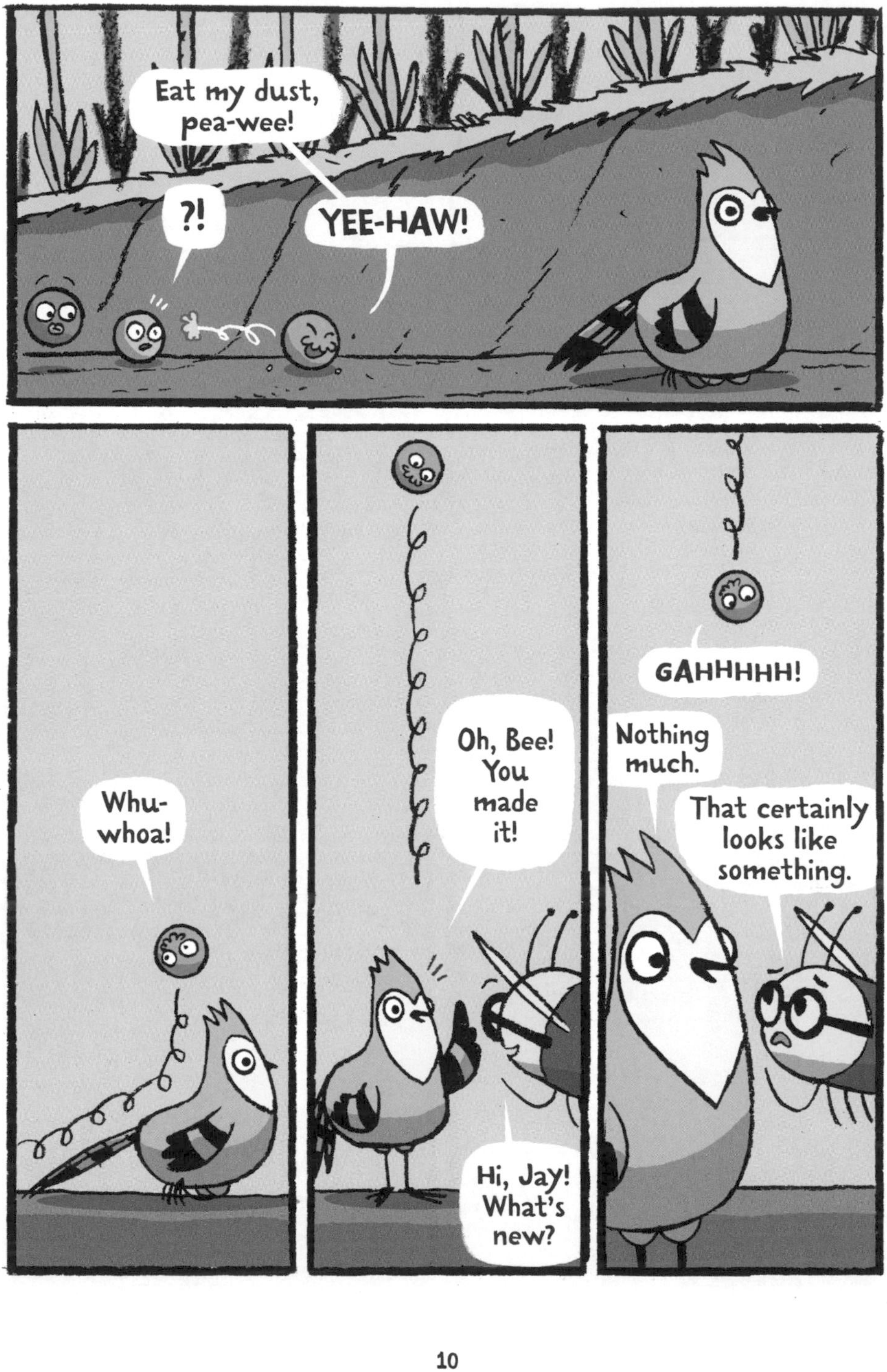
Eat my dust, pea-wee!
?!
YEE-HAW!
Whu-whoa!
Oh, Bee! You made it!
Hi, Jay! What's new?
GAHHHHH!
Nothing much.
That certainly looks like something.

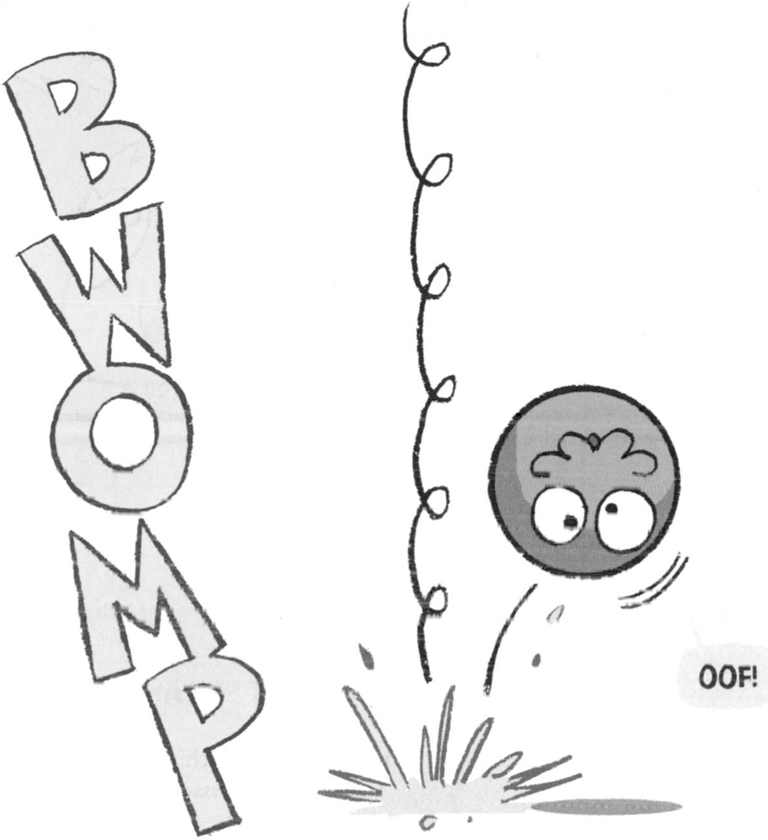
BWOMP
OOF!

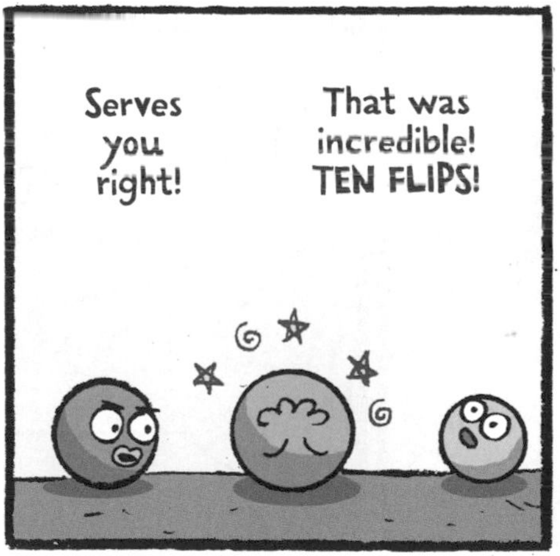
Serves you right!
That was incredible! TEN FLIPS!

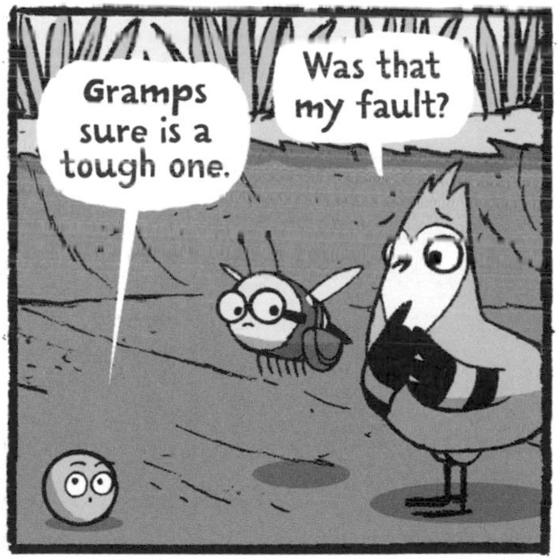
Gramps sure is a tough one.
Was that my fault?

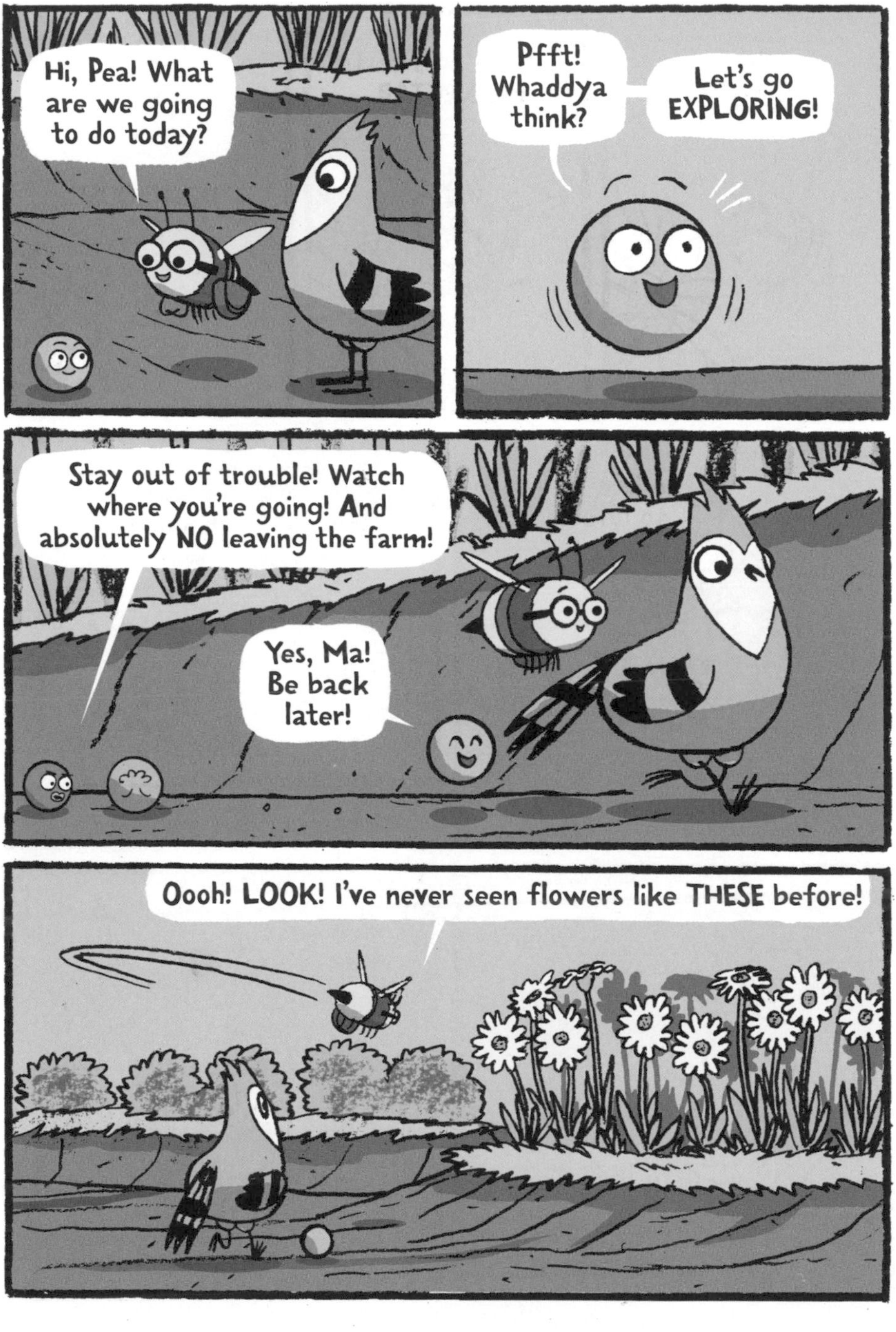
Hi, Pea! What are we going to do today?
Pfft! Whaddya think?
Let's go EXPLORING!
Stay out of trouble! Watch where you're going! And absolutely NO leaving the farm!
Yes, Ma! Be back later!
Oooh! LOOK! I've never seen flowers like THESE before!

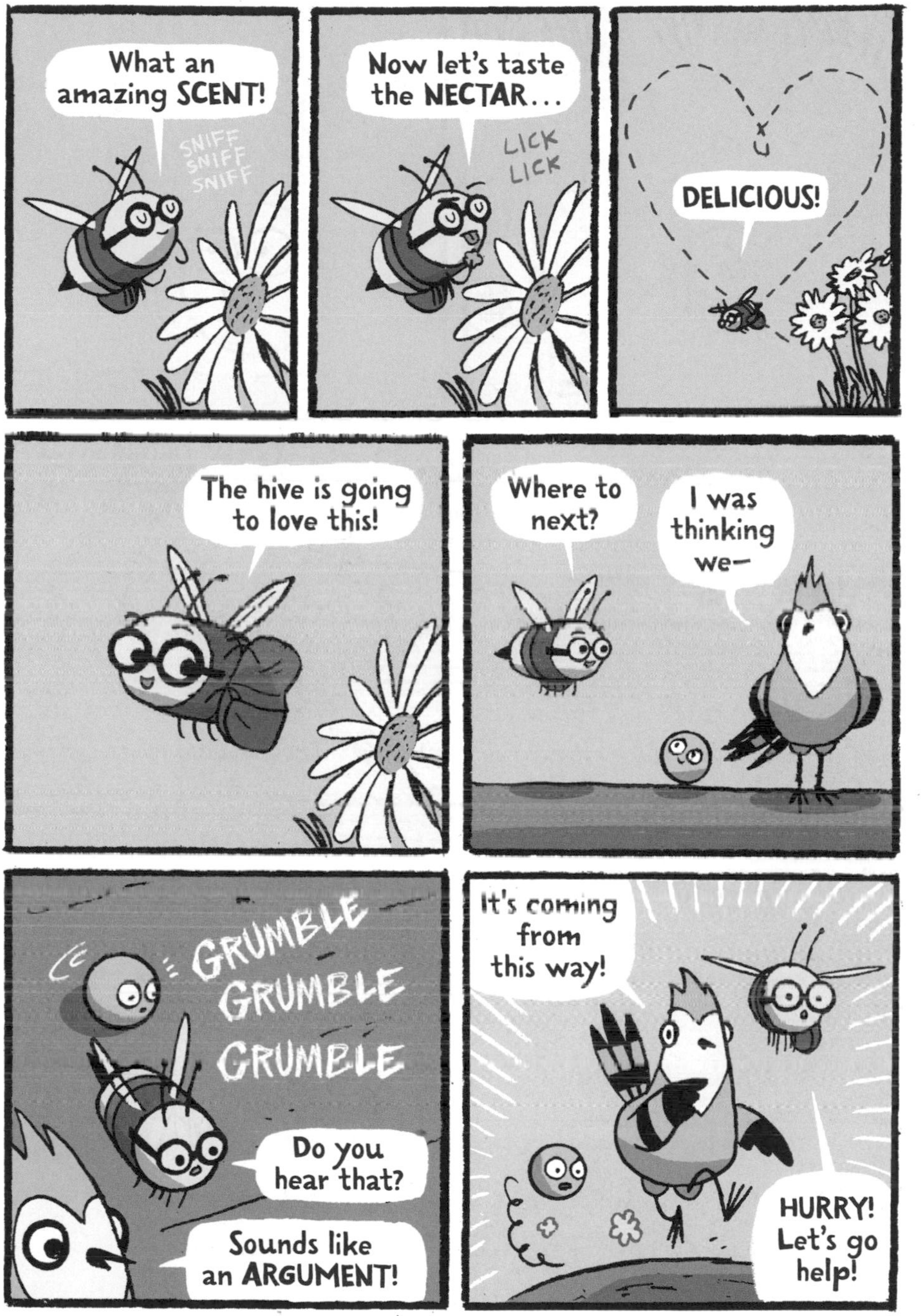

What an amazing SCENT!
SNIFF SNIFF SNIFF
Now let's taste the NECTAR...
LICK LICK
DELICIOUS!
The hive is going to love this!
Where to next?
I was thinking we—
GRUMBLE GRUMBLE GRUMBLE
Do you hear that?
Sounds like an ARGUMENT!
It's coming from this way!
HURRY! Let's go help!

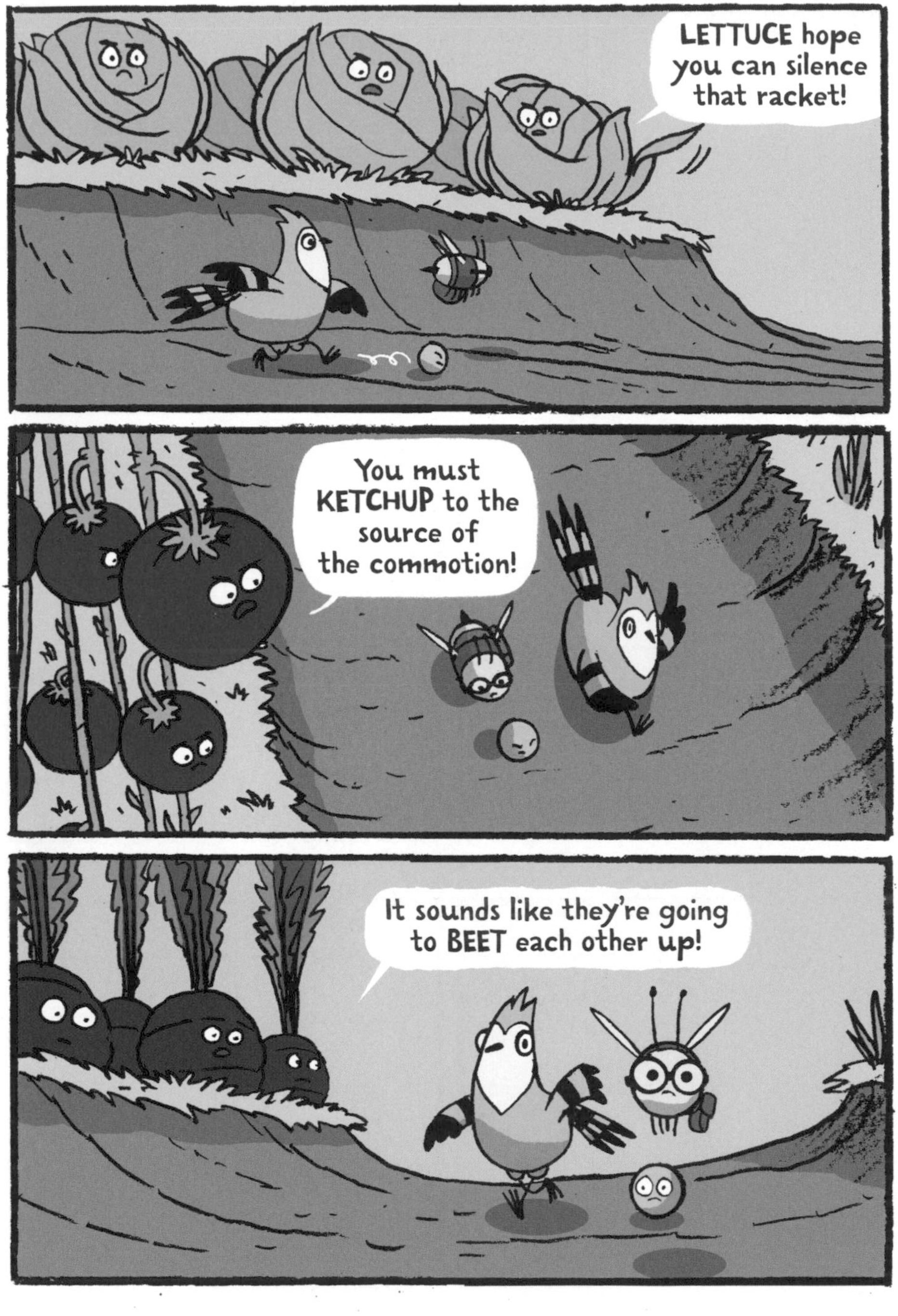
LETTUCE hope you can silence that racket!
You must KETCHUP to the source of the commotion!
It sounds like they're going to BEET each other up!

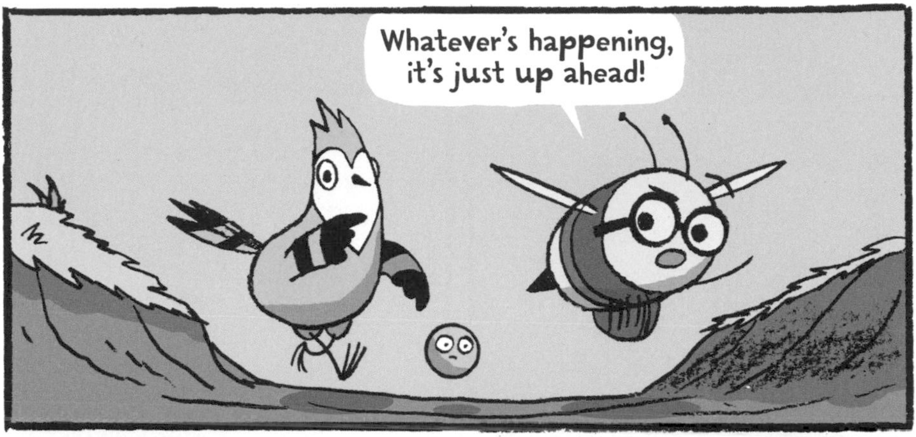
Whatever's happening, it's just up ahead!

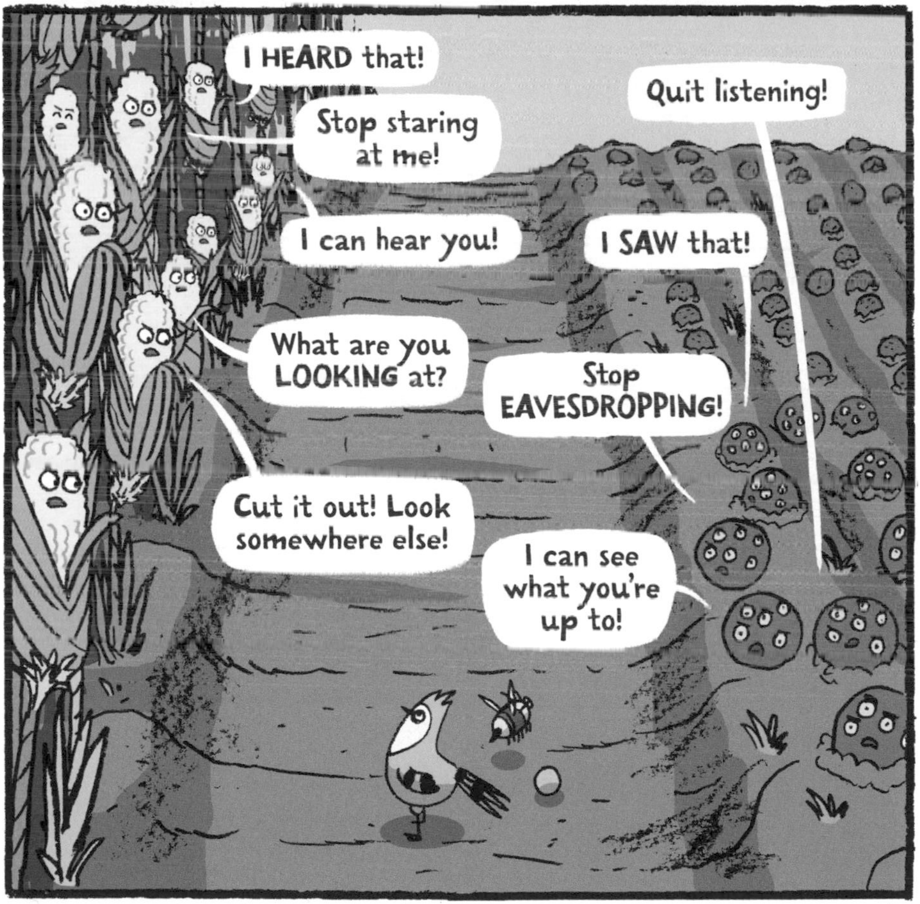
I HEARD that!
Stop staring at me!
I can hear you!
What are you LOOKING at?
Cut it out! Look somewhere else!
Quit listening!
I SAW that!
Stop EAVESDROPPING!
I can see what you're up to!

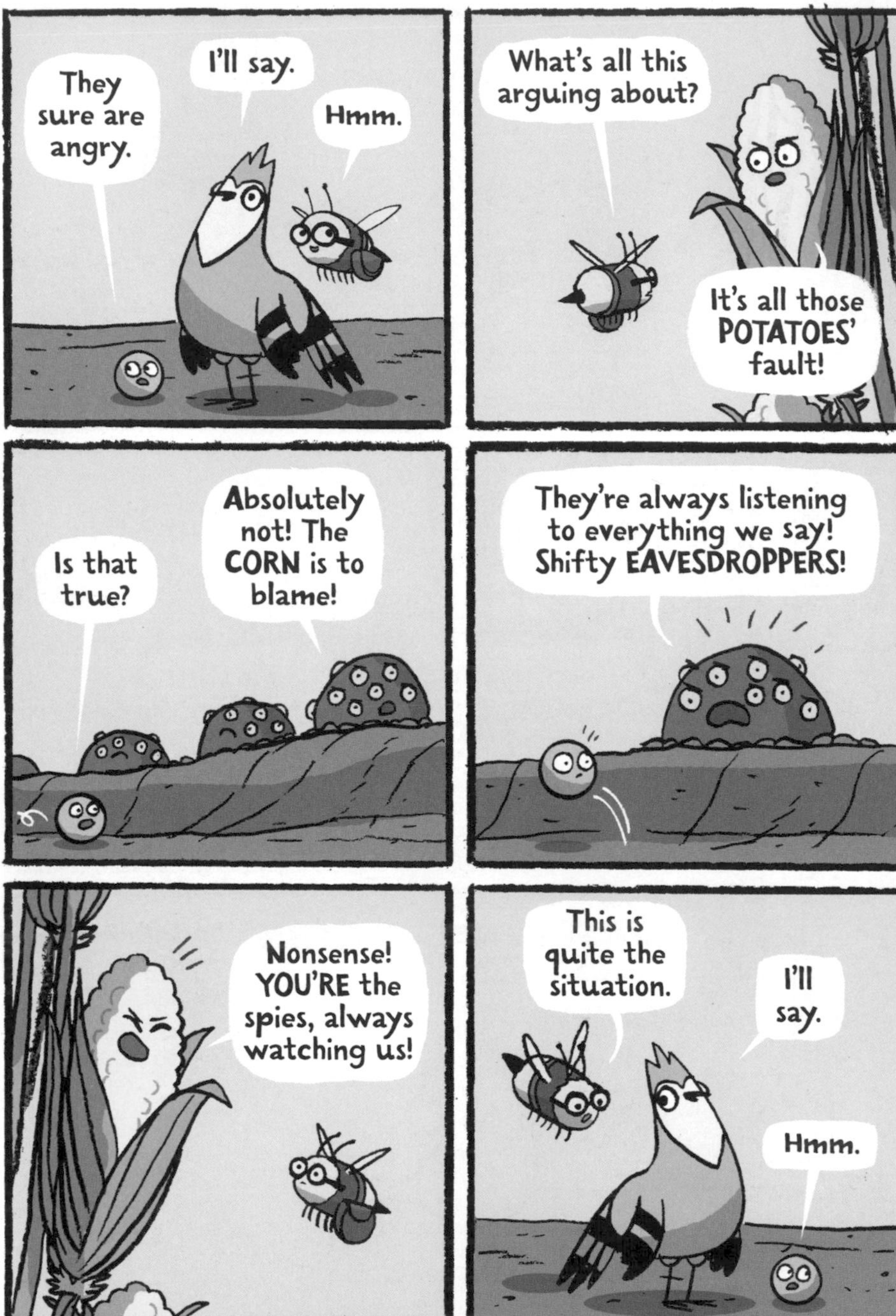
They sure are angry.
I'll say.
Hmm.
What's all this arguing about?
It's all those POTATOES' fault!
Is that true?
Absolutely not! The CORN is to blame!
They're always listening to everything we say! Shifty EAVESDROPPERS!
Nonsense! YOU'RE the spies, always watching us!
This is quite the situation.
I'll say.
Hmm.

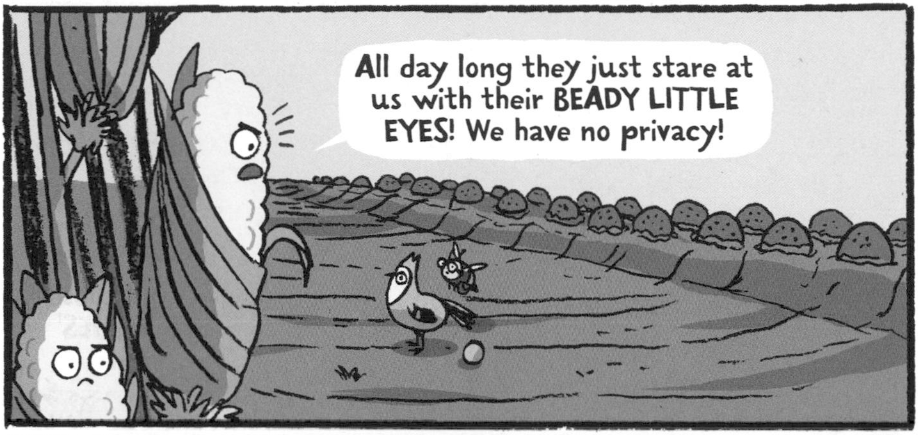
All day long they just stare at us with their BEADY LITTLE EYES! We have no privacy!

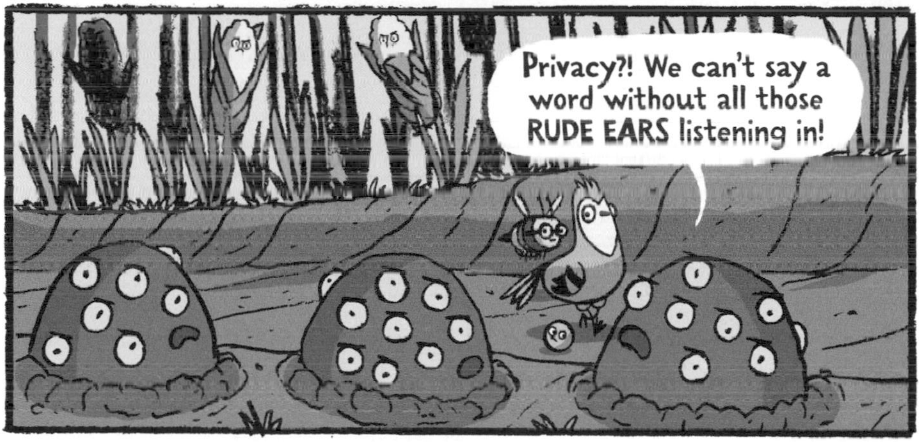
Privacy?! We can't say a word without all those RUDE EARS listening in!

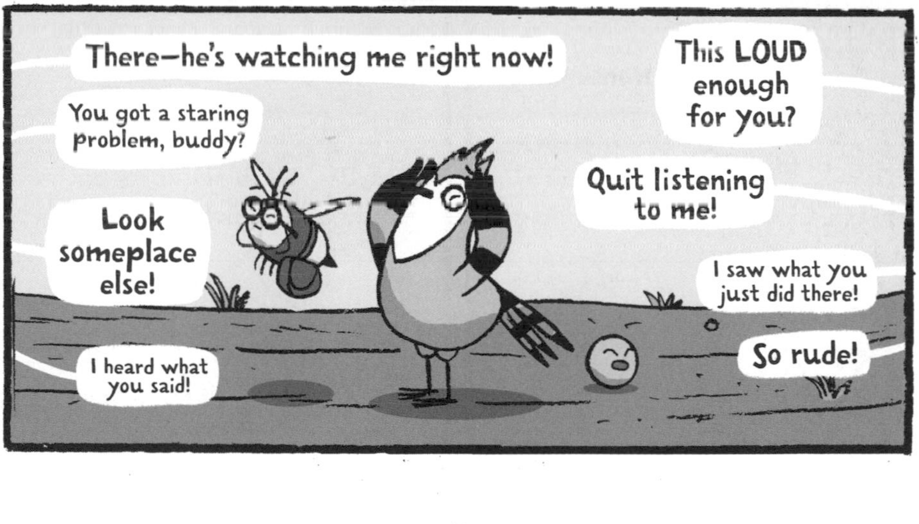
There—he's watching me right now!
This LOUD enough for you?
You got a staring problem, buddy?
Quit listening to me!
Look someplace else!
I saw what you just did there!
I heard what you said!
So rude!

21

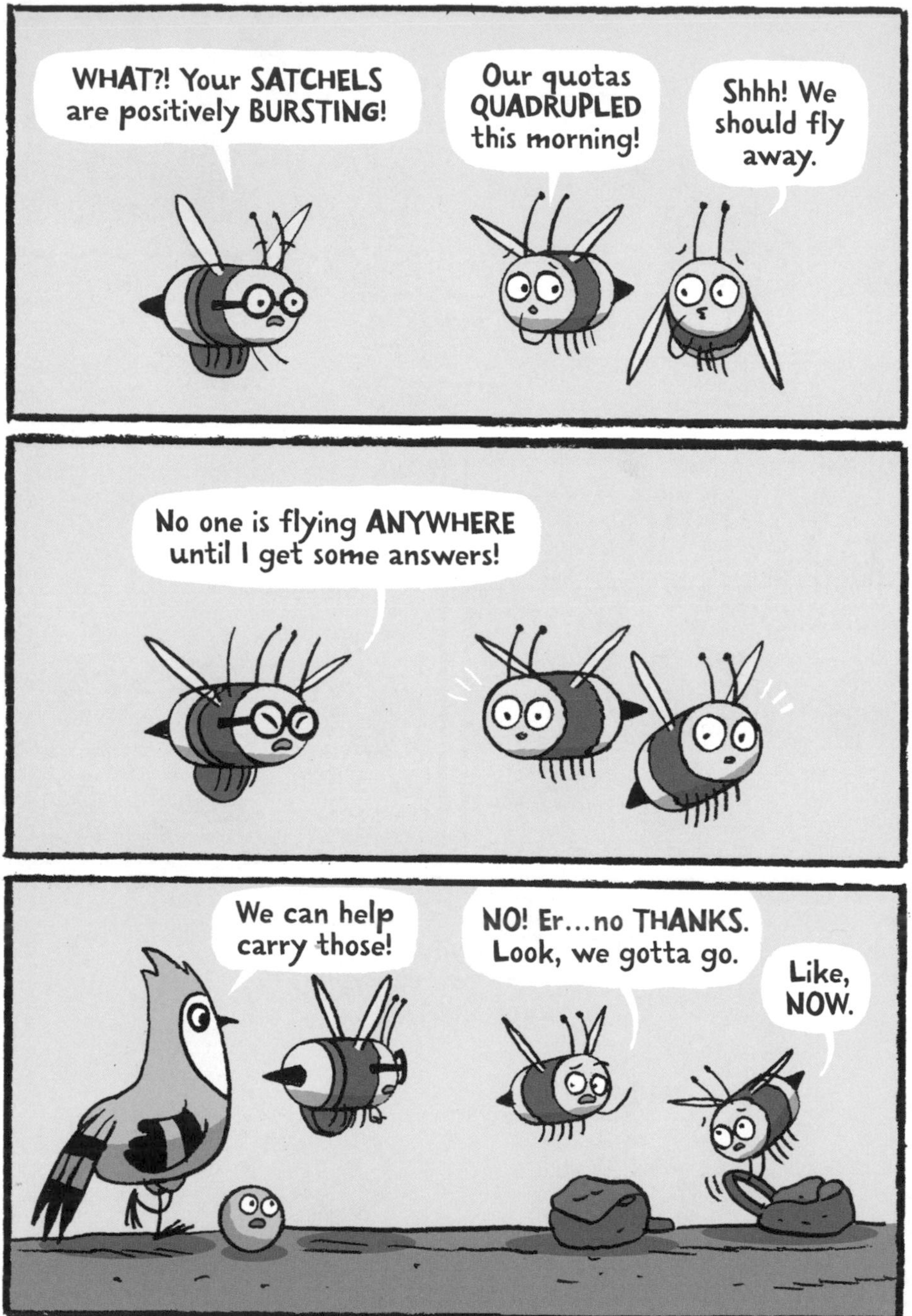
WHAT?! Your SATCHELS are positively BURSTING!
Our quotas QUADRUPLED this morning!
Shhh! We should fly away.
No one is flying ANYWHERE until I get some answers!
We can help carry those!
NO! Er...no THANKS. Look, we gotta go.
Like, NOW.

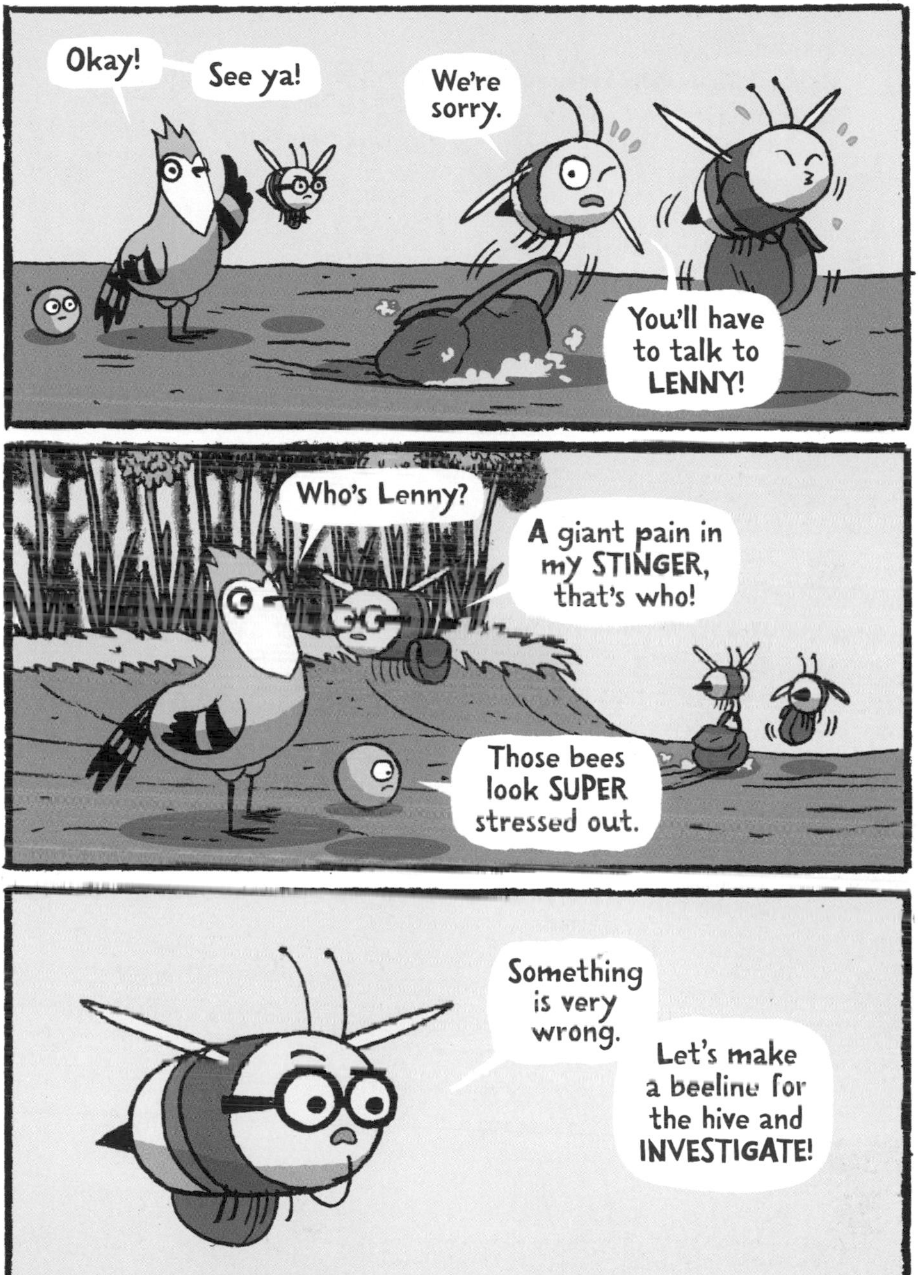
Okay!
See ya!
We're sorry.
You'll have to talk to LENNY!
Who's Lenny?
A giant pain in my STINGER, that's who!
Those bees look SUPER stressed out.
Something is very wrong.
Let's make a beeline for the hive and INVESTIGATE!

24

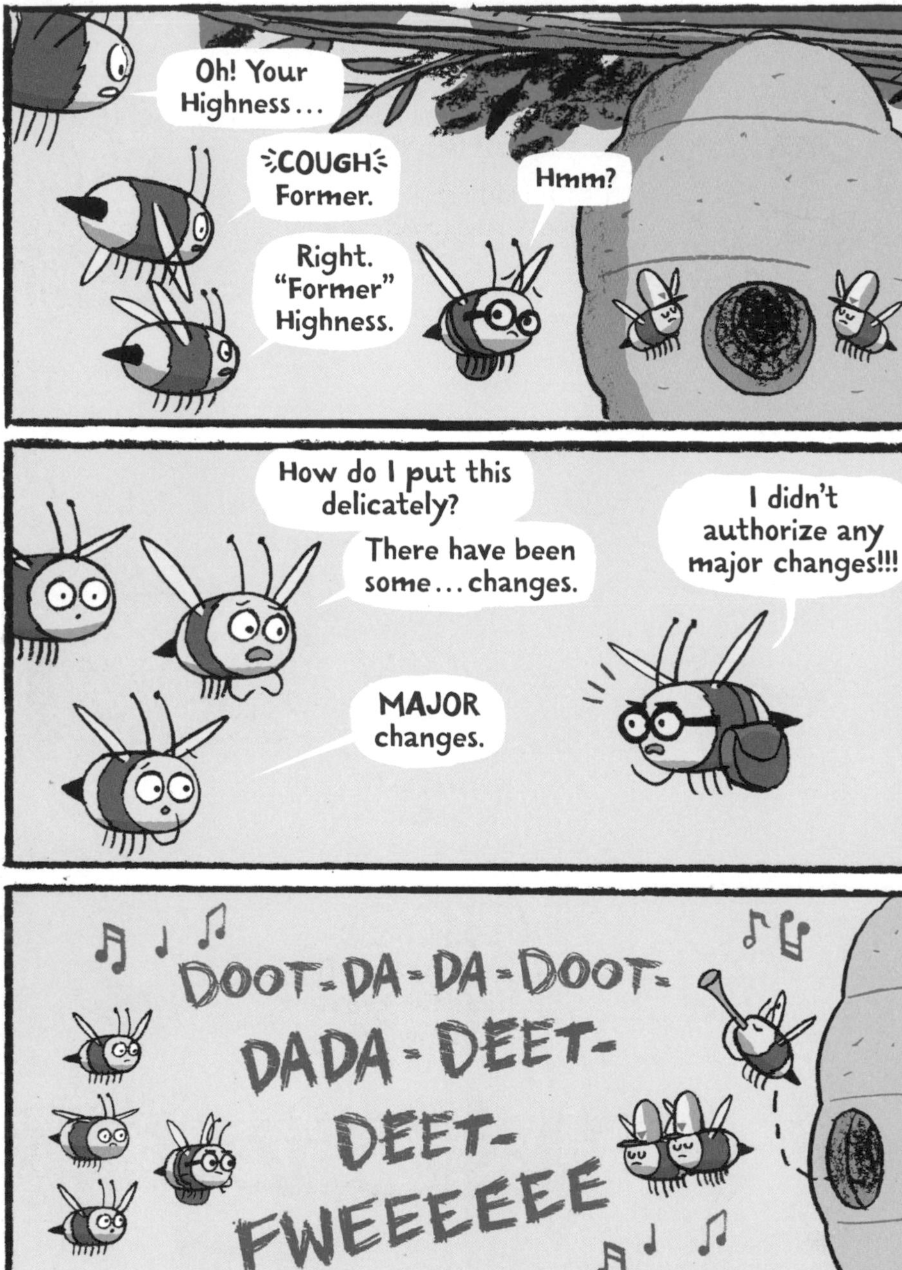
Oh! Your Highness...
COUGH Former.
Hmm?
Right. "Former" Highness.
How do I put this delicately?
There have been some... changes.
I didn't authorize any major changes!!!
MAJOR changes.
DOOT-DA-DA-DOOT-DADA-DEET-DEET-FWEEEEEE

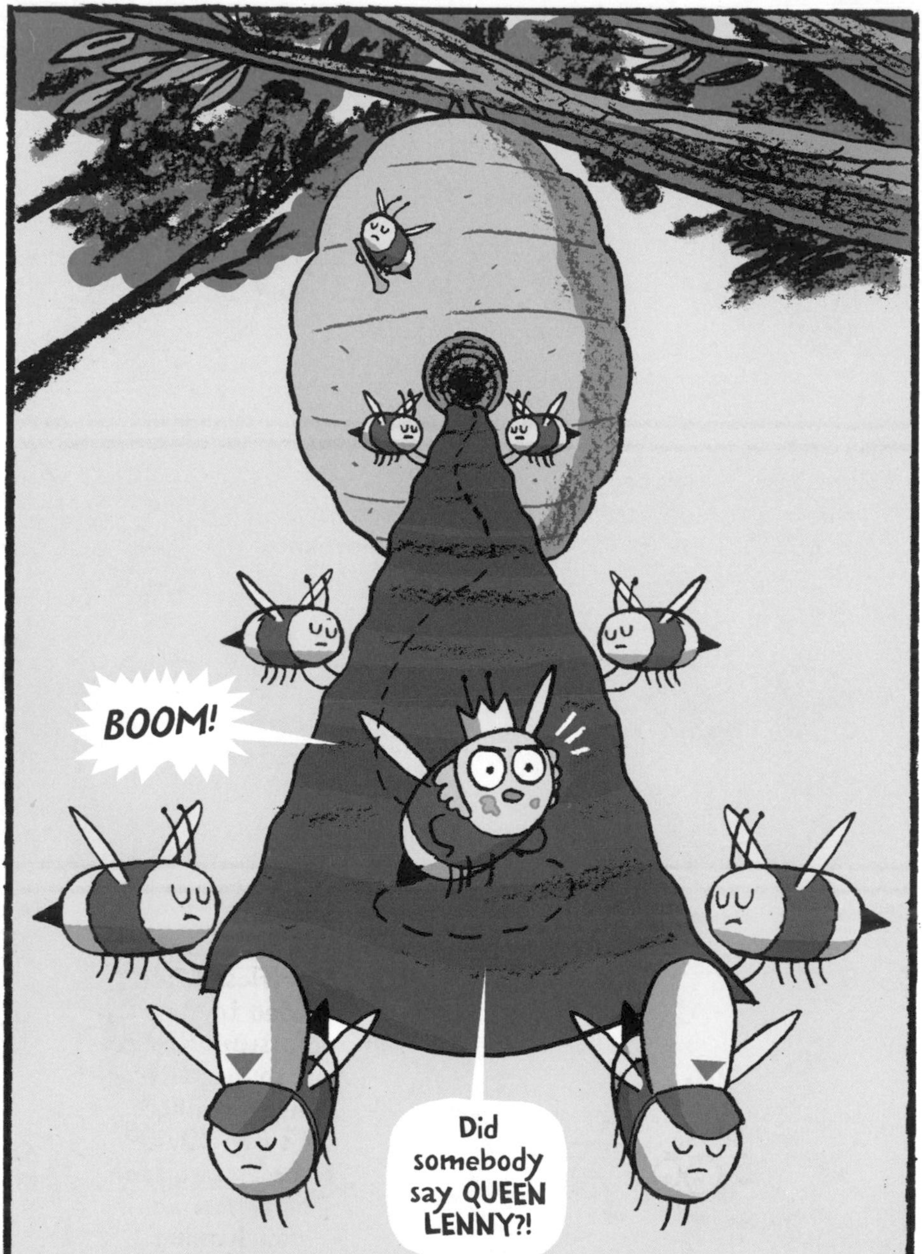
BOOM!
Did somebody say QUEEN LENNY?!

29

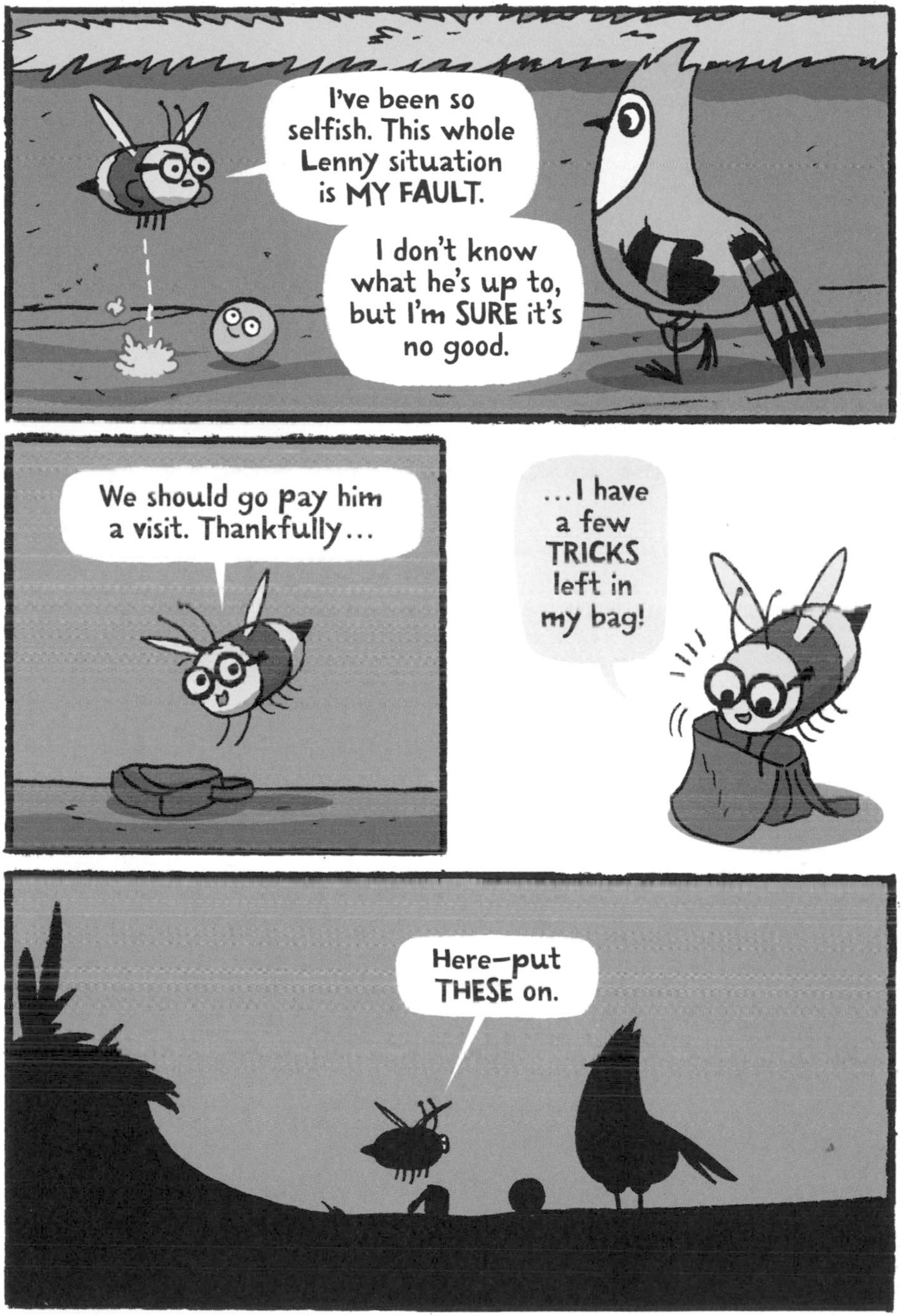
I've been so selfish. This whole Lenny situation is MY FAULT.
I don't know what he's up to, but I'm SURE it's no good.
We should go pay him a visit. Thankfully...
...I have a few TRICKS left in my bag!
Here—put THESE on.

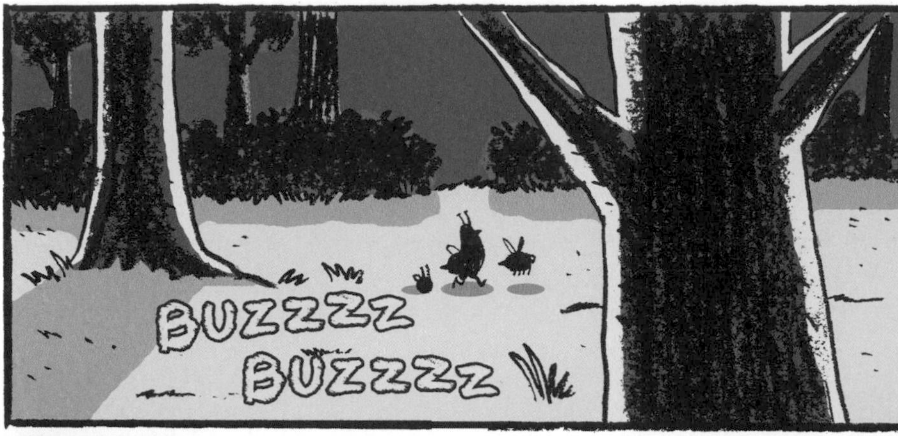
BUZZZZ
BUZZZZ

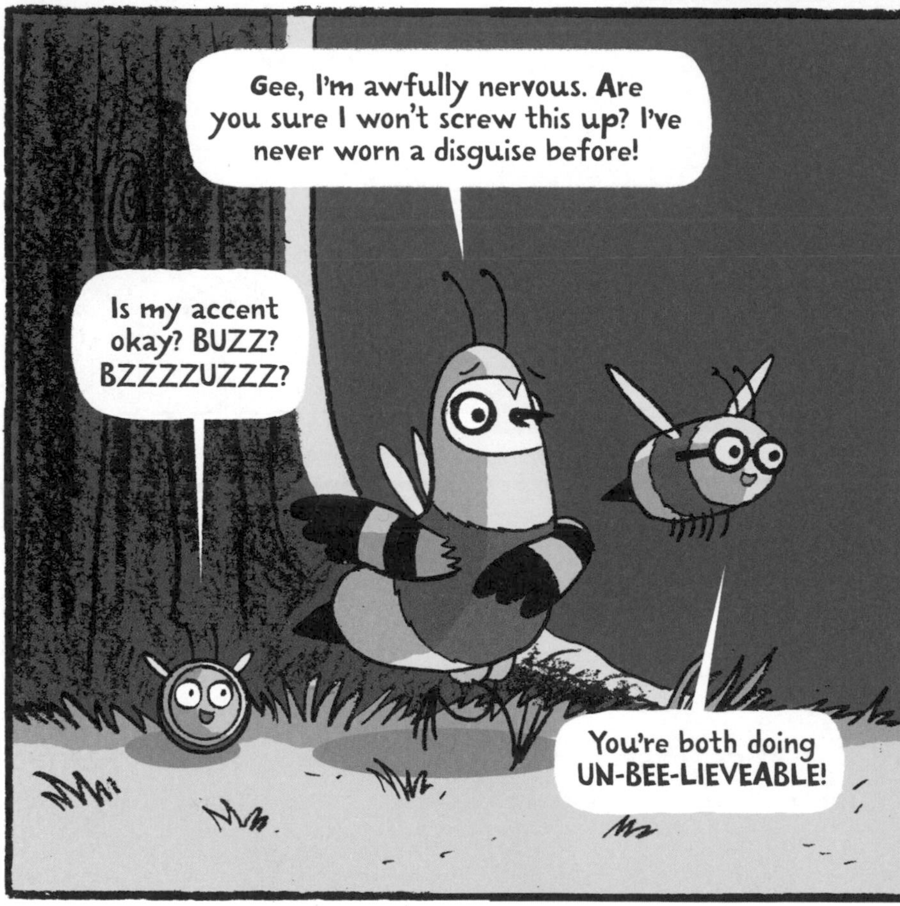
Gee, I'm awfully nervous. Are you sure I won't screw this up? I've never worn a disguise before!
Is my accent okay? BUZZ? BZZZZUZZZ?
You're both doing UN-BEE-LIEVEABLE!

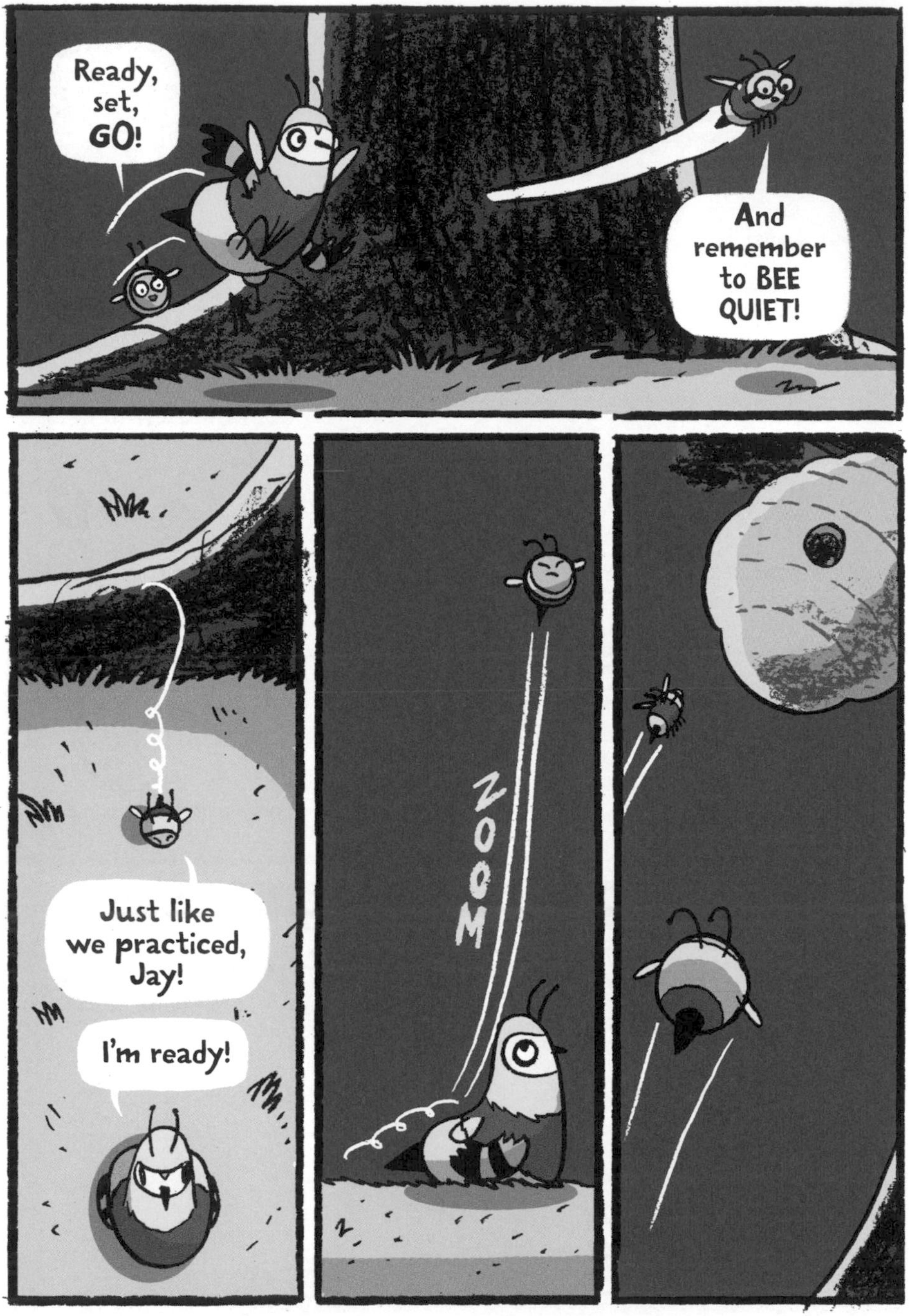
Ready, set, GO!
And remember to BEE QUIET!
Just like we practiced, Jay!
I'm ready!
ZOOM

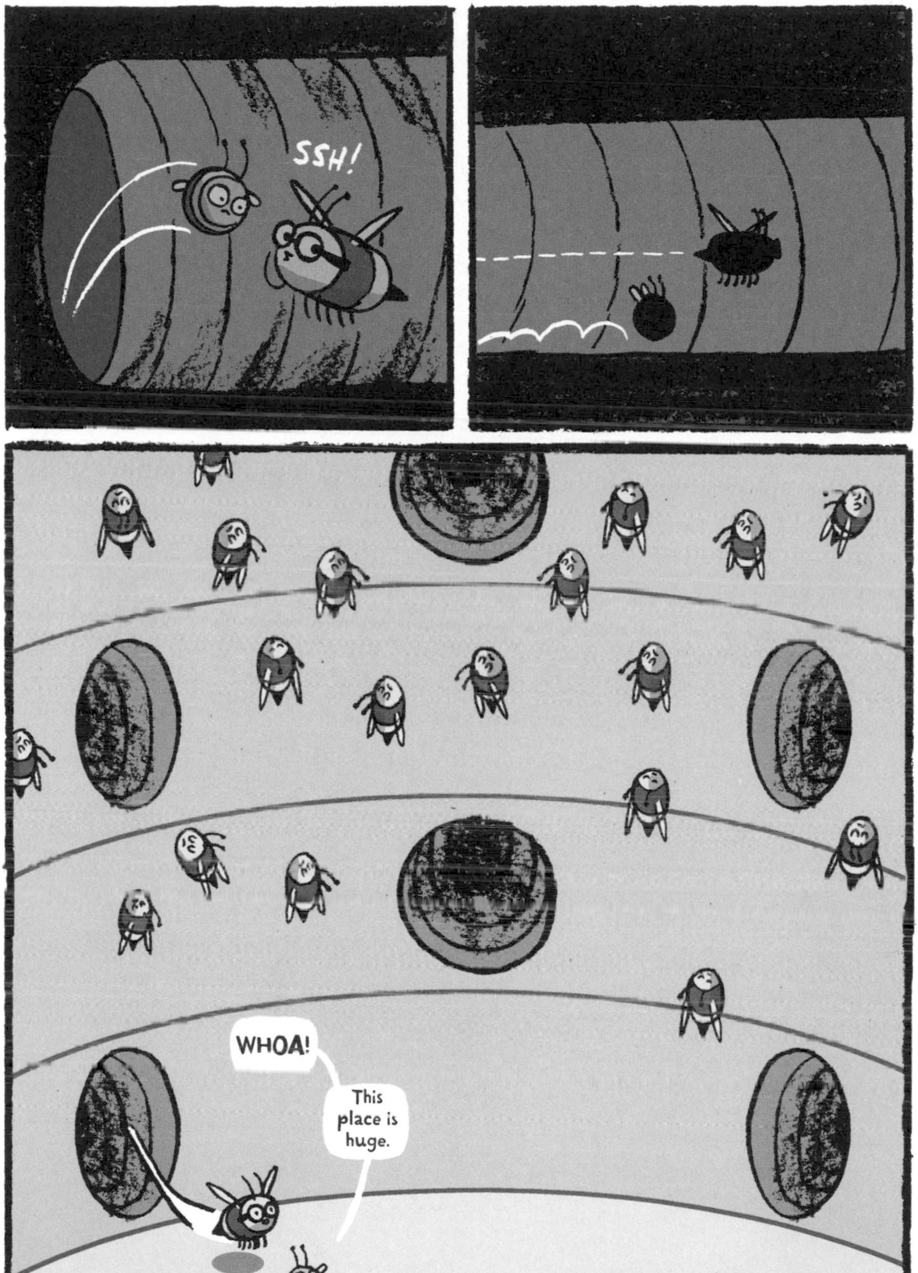
SSH!
WHOA!
This place is huge.

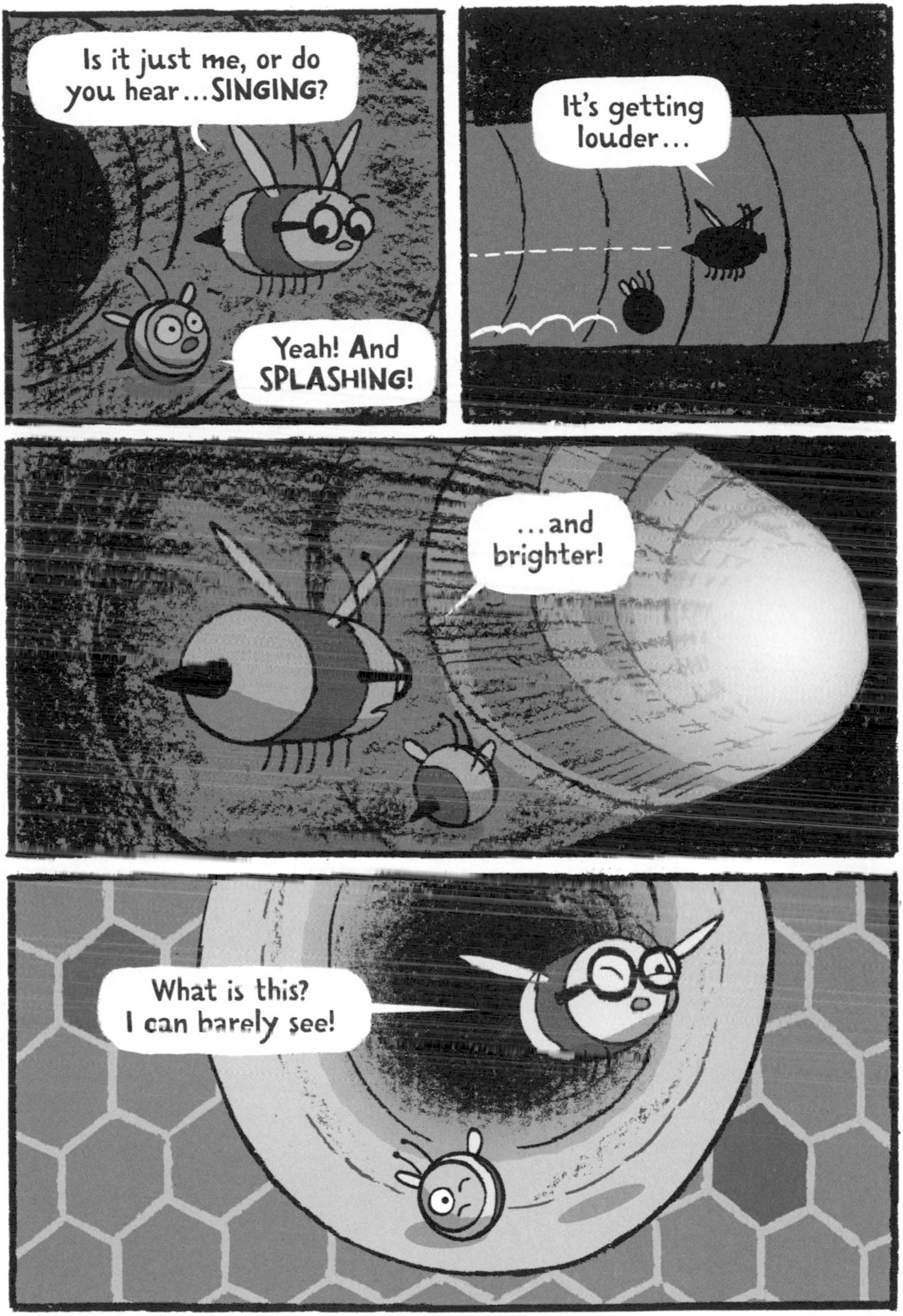
Is it just me, or do you hear...SINGING?
Yeah! And SPLASHING!
It's getting louder...
...and brighter!
What is this? I can barely see!

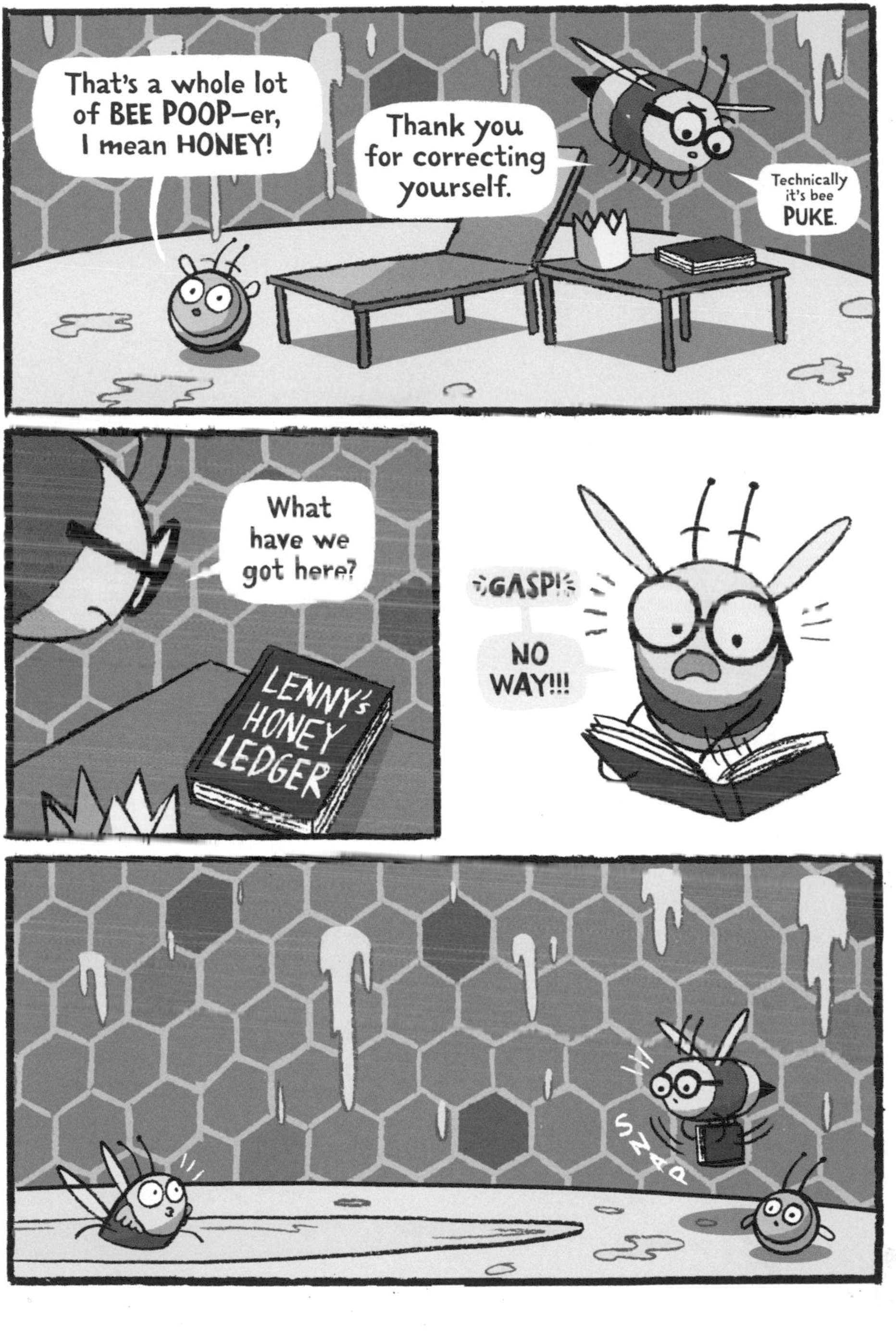
That's a whole lot of BEE POOP—er, I mean HONEY!
Thank you for correcting yourself.
Technically it's bee PUKE.
What have we got here?
LENNY's HONEY LEDGER
GASP!
NO WAY!!!
SZAP

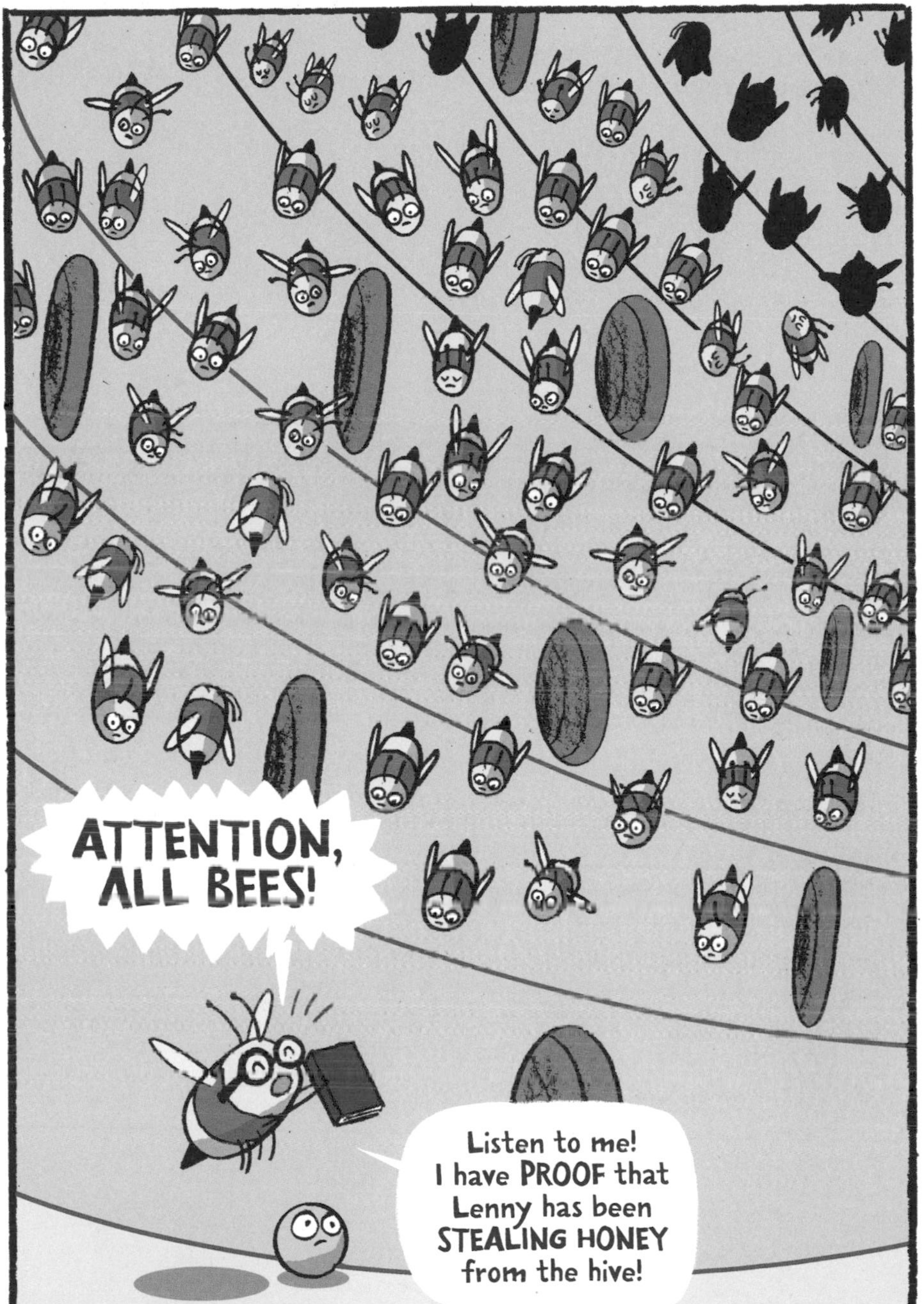
ATTENTION, ALL BEES!
Listen to me! I have PROOF that Lenny has been STEALING HONEY from the hive!

44

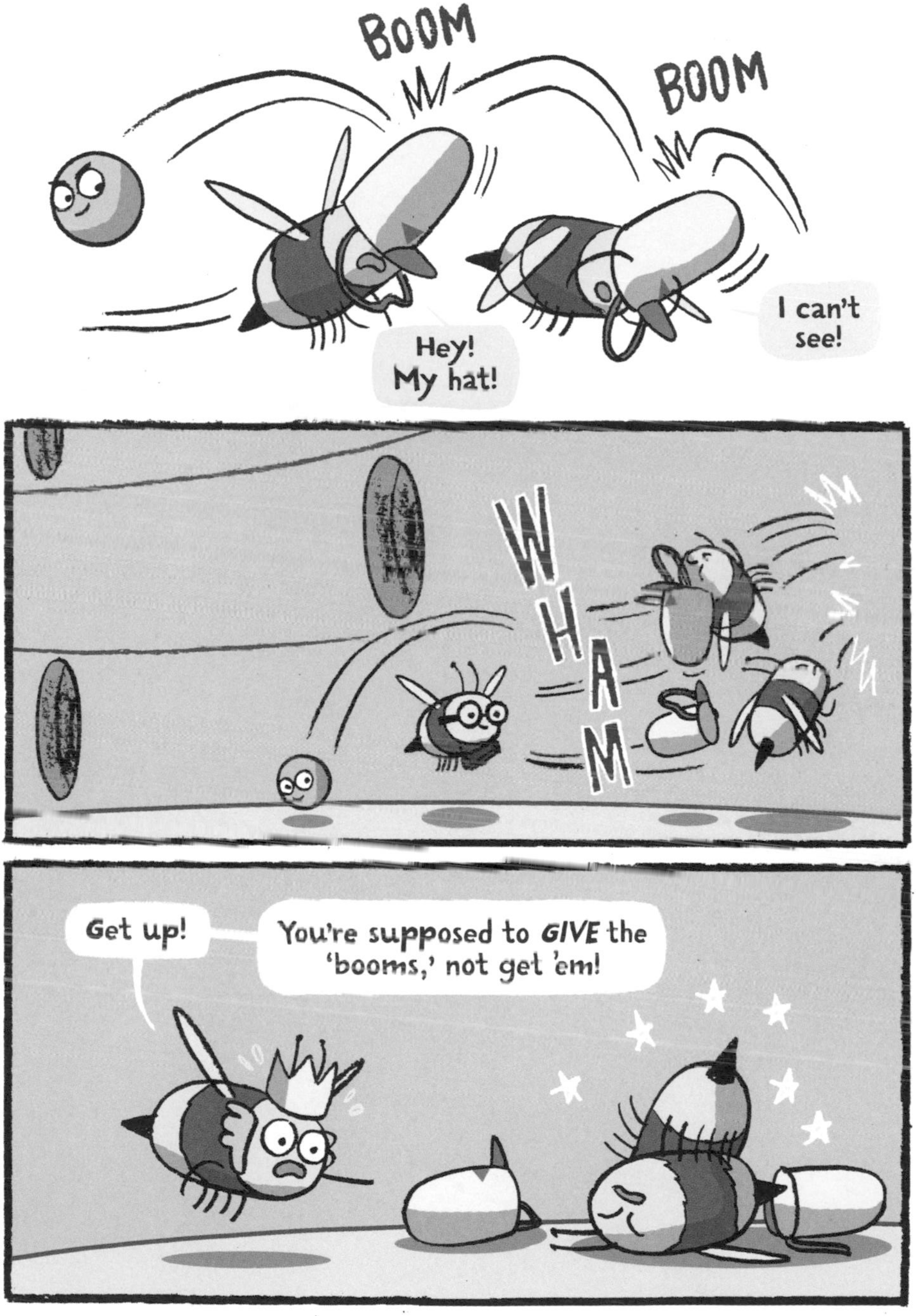
BOOM
BOOM
Hey! My hat!
I can't see!
WHAM
Get up!
You're supposed to *GIVE* the 'booms,' not get 'em!

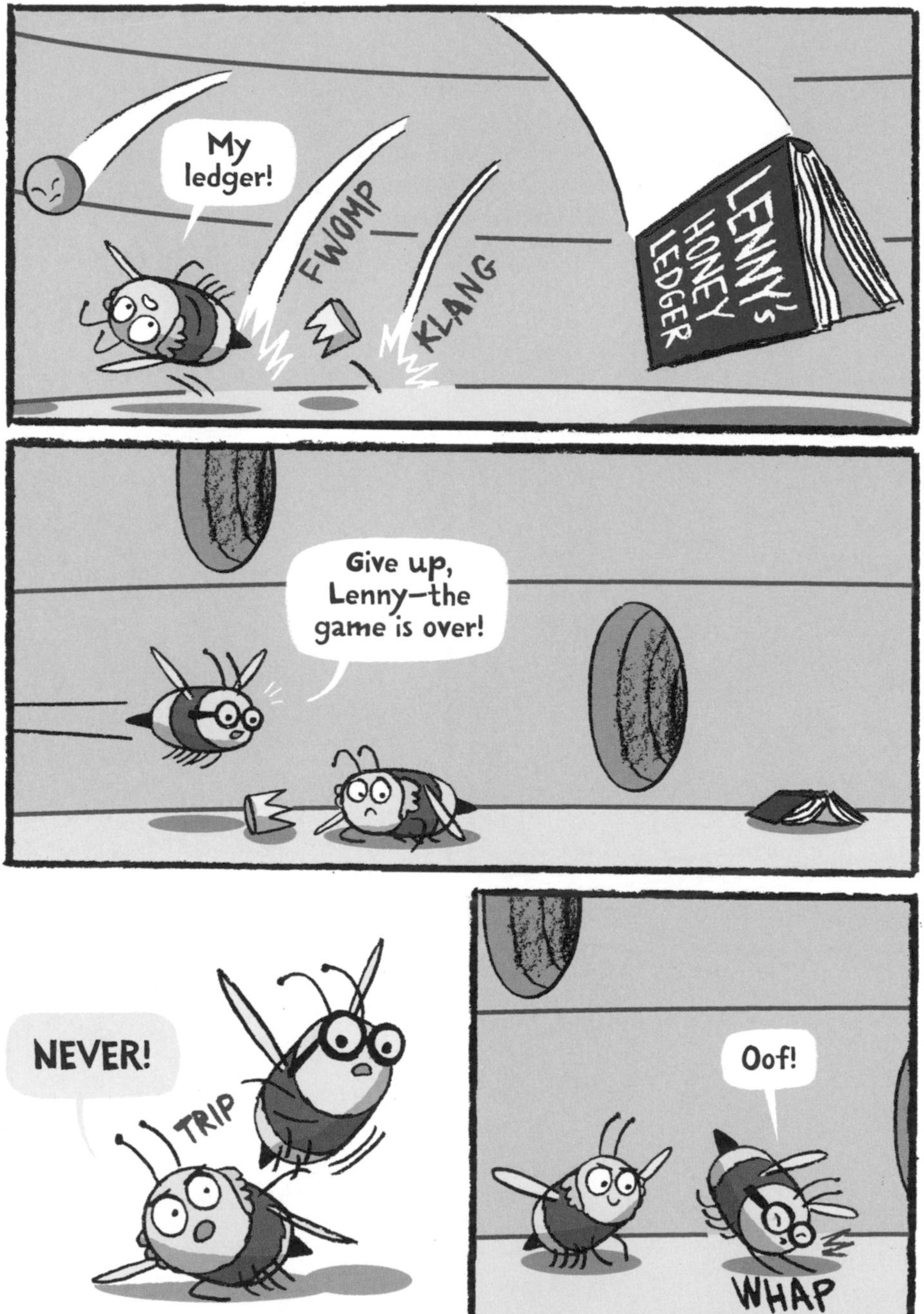
My ledger!
FWOMP
KLANG
LENNY'S HONEY LEDGER
Give up, Lenny—the game is over!
NEVER!
TRIP
Oof!
WHAP

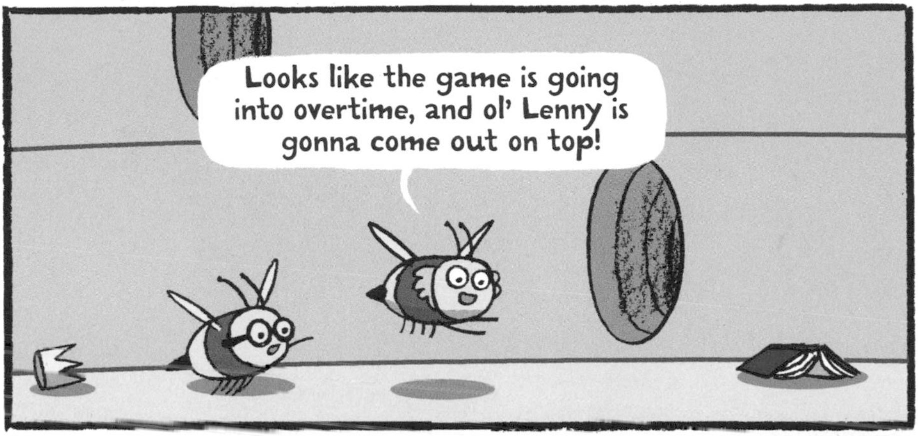
Looks like the game is going into overtime, and ol' Lenny is gonna come out on top!

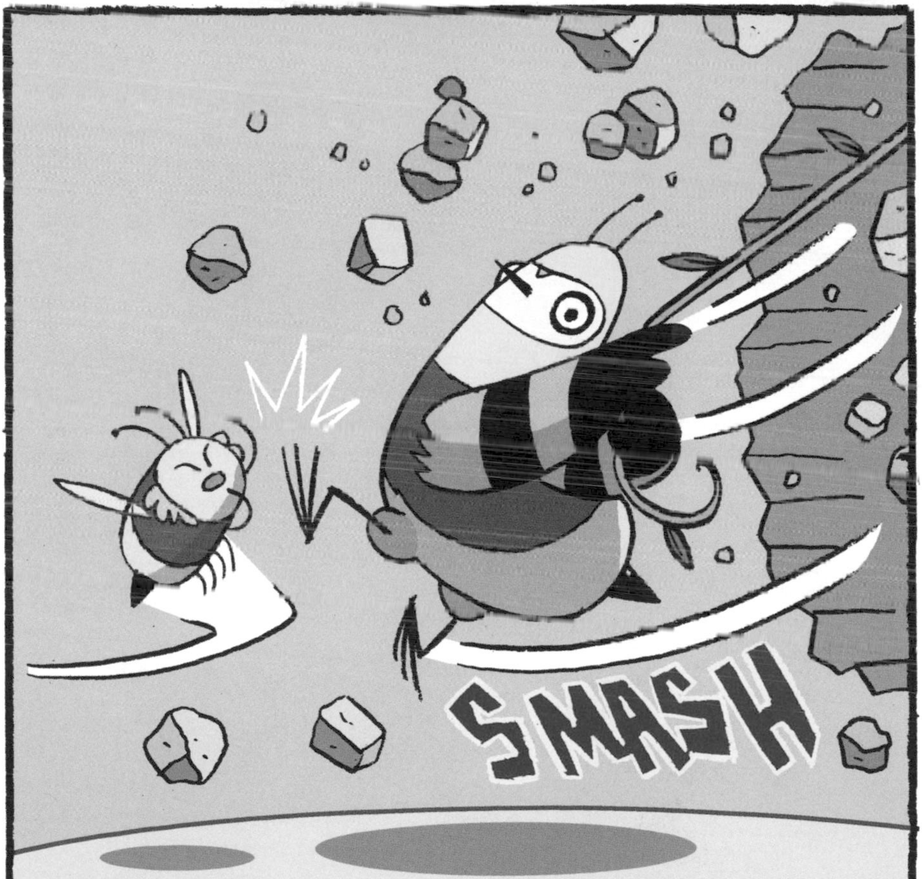
SMASH

51

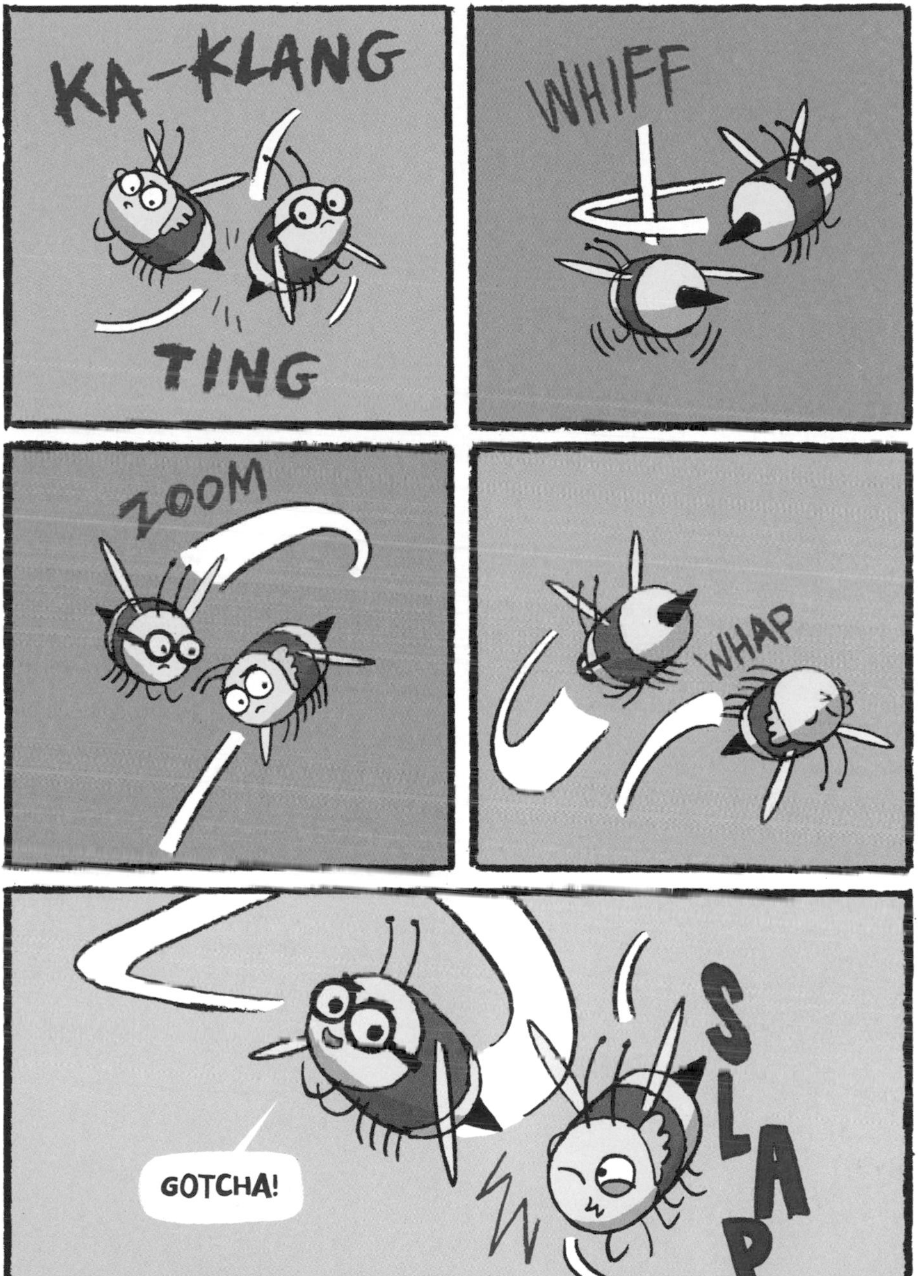
KA-KLANG
TING
WHIFF
ZOOM
WHAP
GOTCHA!
SLAP

54

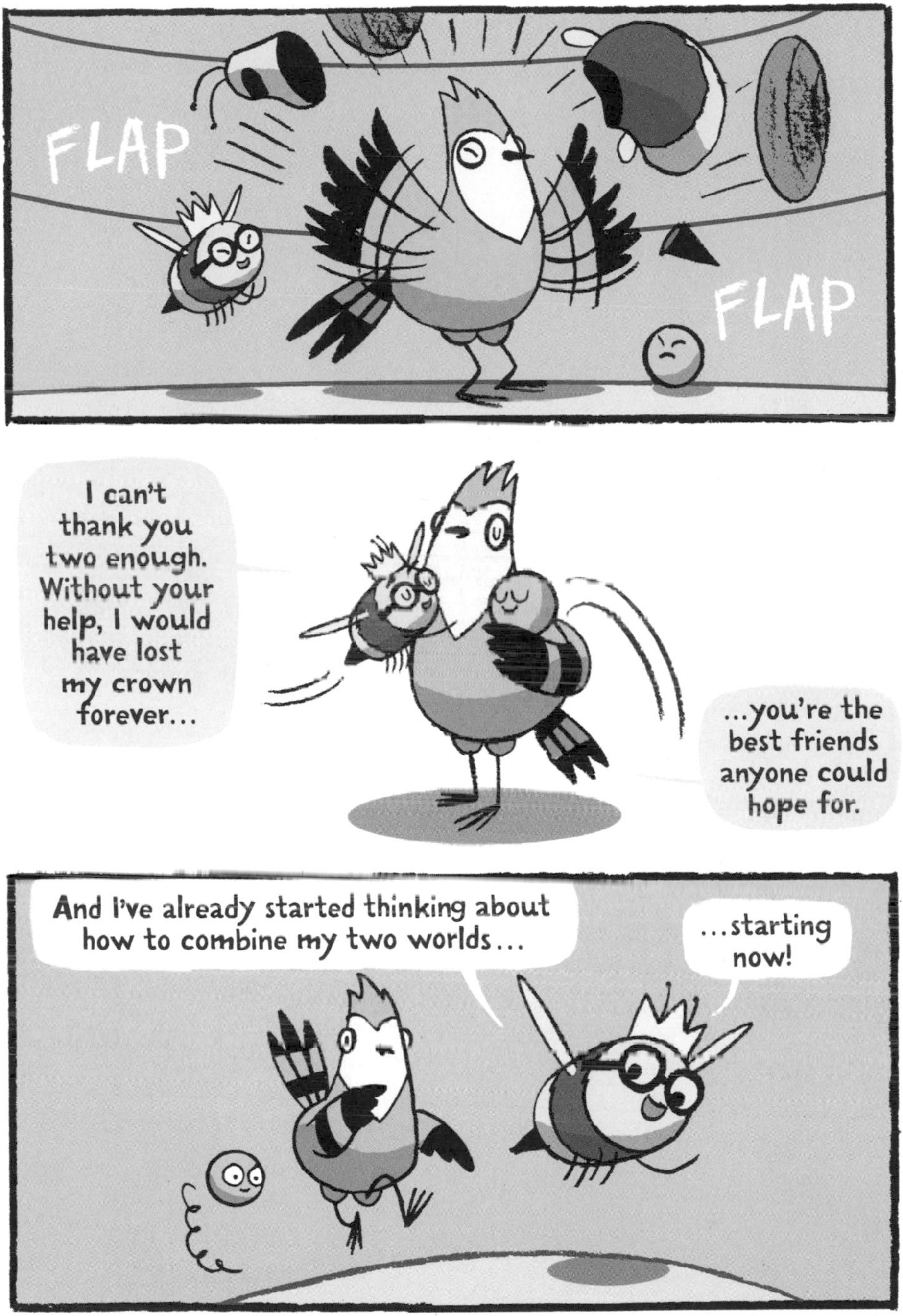
FLAP
FLAP
I can't thank you two enough. Without your help, I would have lost my crown forever...
...you're the best friends anyone could hope for.
And I've already started thinking about how to combine my two worlds...
...starting now!

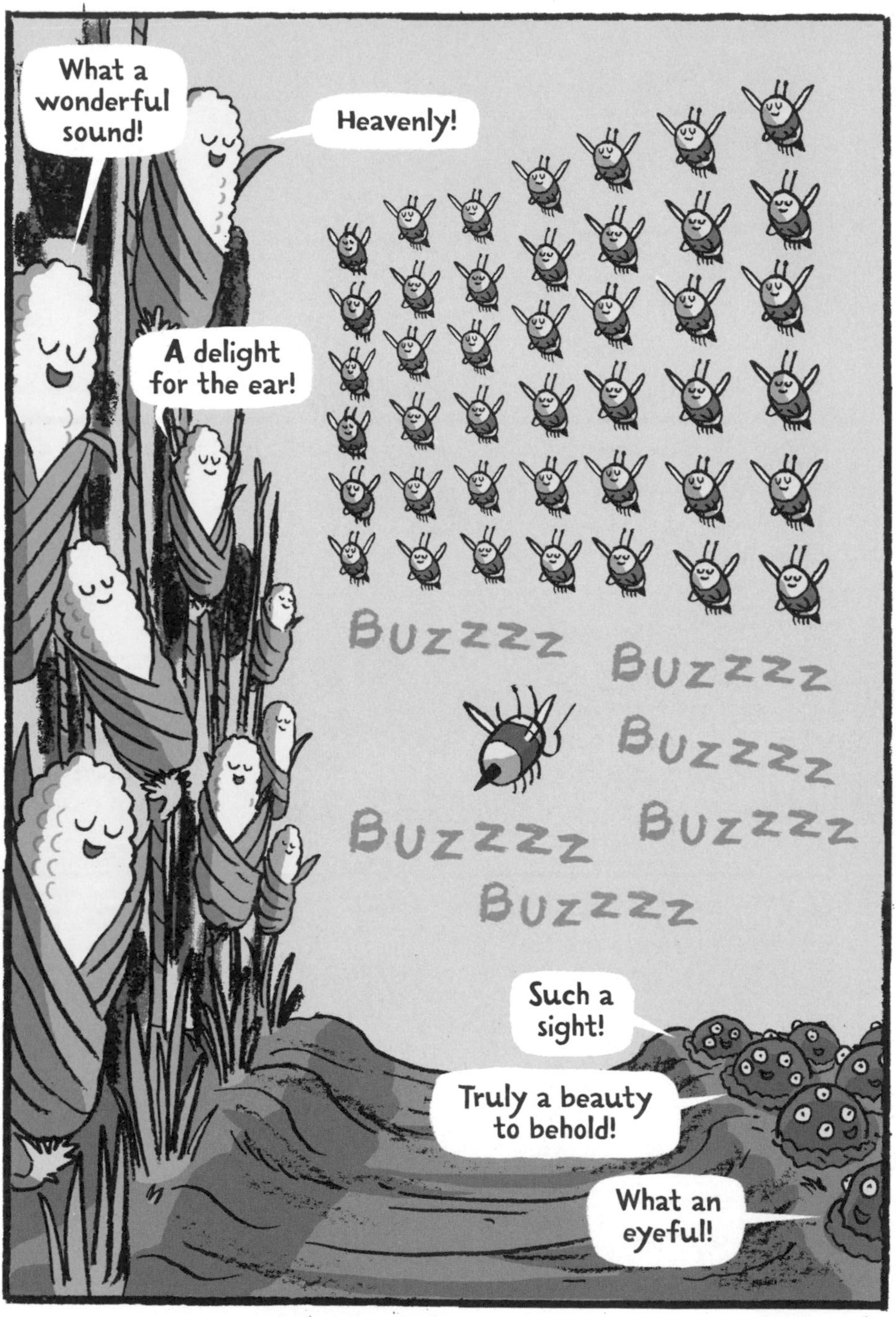
What a wonderful sound!
Heavenly!
A delight for the ear!
BUZZZZ
BUZZZZ
BUZZZZ
BUZZZZ
BUZZZZ
BUZZZZ
Such a sight!
Truly a beauty to behold!
What an eyeful!

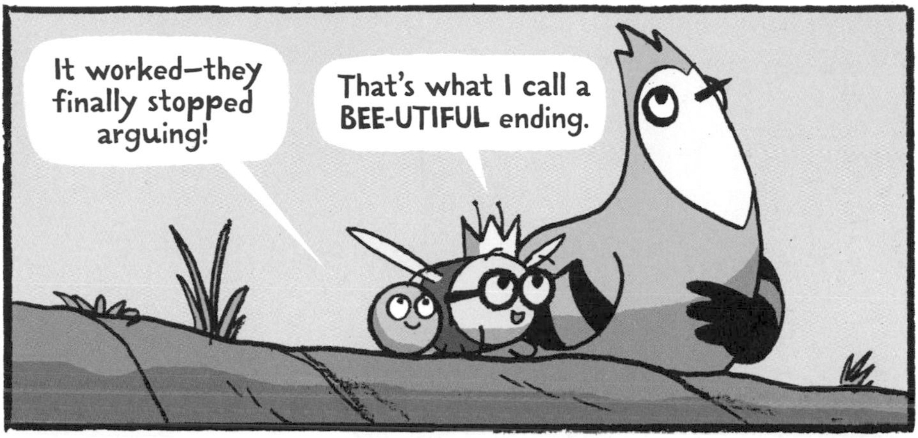
It worked—they finally stopped arguing!
That's what I call a BEE-UTIFUL ending.

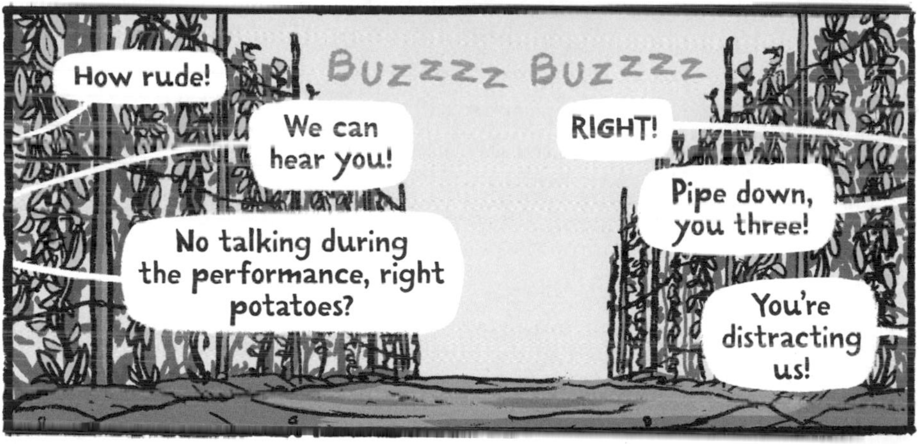
BUZZZZ BUZZZZ
How rude!
We can hear you!
No talking during the performance, right potatoes?
RIGHT!
Pipe down, you three!
You're distracting us!

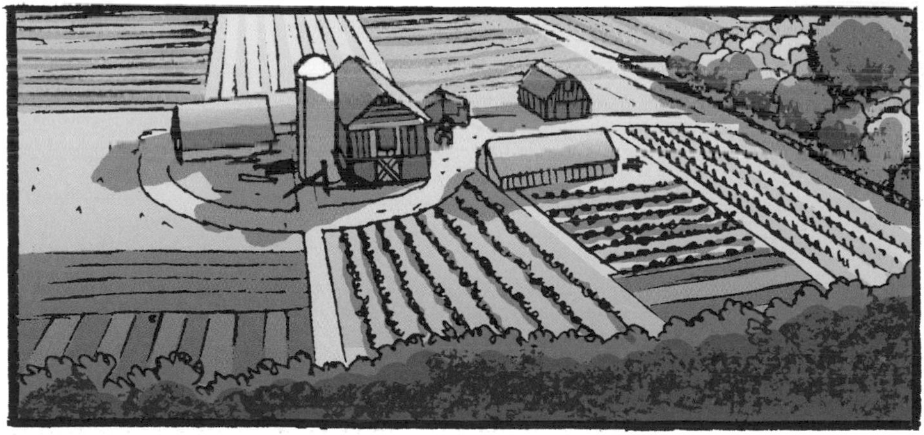

Thank you to Bret Parks, Juliet Parks, Elise Parks,
Robin Parks, and Ssalefish Comics, without whom
this book would not have been possible.

HarperAlley is an imprint of HarperCollins Publishers.

Pea, Bee, & Jay #2: Wannabees
Copyright © 2020 by Brian Smith
All rights reserved. Printed in Slovenia.
No part of this book may be used or reproduced in any manner whatsoever without written permission
except in the case of brief quotations embodied in critical articles and reviews. For information address
HarperCollins Children's Books, a division of HarperCollins Publishers, 195 Broadway, New York, NY 10007.
www.harperalley.com

Library of Congress Control Number: 2020931680
ISBN 978-0-06-298120-2 — ISBN 978-0-06-298119-6 (pbk.)

The artist used pencils, paper, a computer, and bee poop (lots and lots
of bee poop) to create the digital illustrations for this book.
Typography by Erica De Chavez and Andrew Arnold
20 21 22 23 24   GPS   10 9 8 7 6 5 4 3 2 1
❖
First Edition